Dear Readers,

I still remember the first time I read Donald Goines, the godfather of street lit. He was the first to write books about characters I could identify with. To some, the stories may have been aggressive, overly stylized, and even dangerous. But there was an honesty there—a realness. I made a vow that if I wrote a book or got into the publishing game, I would try the same one-two punch—that of a *Daddy Cool* or *Black Gangster*.

In 2005, my memoir, *From Pieces to Weight*, marked the beginning. Now I'm rounding up some of the top writers, same way I rounded up some of the top rappers in the game, to form **G-Unit** and take this series to the top of the literary world. The stories in the **G-Unit** series are the kinds of dramas me and my crew have been dealing with our whole lives: death, deceit, double-crosses, ultimate loyalty, and total betrayal. It's about our life on the streets, and no one knows it better than us. Not to mention, when it comes to delivering authentic gritty urban stories of the high and low life, our audience expects the best.

That's what we're going to deliver, with **K'wan**, bestselling author of *Gangsta* and *Hood Rat*; **Mark Anthony**, bestselling author of *Paper Chasers* and *The Take Down*; and **Relentless Aaron**, author of *Push* and *The Last Kingpin*.

You know, I don't do anything halfway, and we're going to take this street lit thing to a whole other level. Are you ready?

G Unit
Books

NEW YORK LONDON TORONTO SYDNEY

HARLEM HEAT

50 Cent
and Mark Anthony

Pocket Books
A Division of Simon & Schuster, Inc.
1230 Avenue of the Americas
New York, NY 10020

First G-Unit/MTV/Pocket Books trade paperback edition July 2007

POCKET BOOKS and colophon are registered trademarks of Simon & Schuster, Inc.

For information about special discounts for bulk purchases, please contact Simon & Schuster Special Sales at 1-800-456-6798 or business@simonandschuster.com

Manufactured in the United States of America

10 9 8 7 6 5 4 3 2 1

ISBN-13: 978-1-4165-4909-3
ISBN-10:   1-4165-4909-9

*This book is dedicated to my father, Lee,
my first real-life example of an
entrepreneur.*

Acknowledgments

I first have to thank my fellow Queens, New York native, 50 Cent, for giving me the opportunity to participate in this G-Unit series of books. To my agent, Marc Gerald, I thank you for connecting the dots; after eight years we finally hooked up. To my editor Lauren, you are the easiest to work with. Thank you for your professionalism. To that great man who taught me that *I don't have to chase after what I can attract*, this book is living proof of that. I thank you for that jewel. Nikki Turner, K'Wan, K. Elliott, Noire, and Relentless Aaron, let's keep making it happen! To all of my readers, thank you for supporting me. My imagination is limitless and there will definitely be more hot books to follow this one!

1

Fast Forward to
September 2006
Long Island, New York

𝕴 can't front. I was nervous as hell. My heart was thumping a mile a minute, like it was about to jump outta my chest. The same god-damn state trooper had now been following us for more than three exits and I knew that it was just a matter of seconds before he was gonna turn on his lights and pull us over. So I put on my signal and switched lanes and prepared to exit the parkway, hoping that he would change his mind about stop-ping us.

"Chyna, what the fuck are you doing?" my moms asked me as she fidgeted in her seat.

"Ma, you know this nigga is gonna pull us over, so I'm just acting like I'm purposely exiting before he pulls us over. It'll be easier to play shit off if he does stop us."

"Chyna, I swear to God you gonna get us locked the fuck up. Just relax and drive!" my mother barked as she turned her head to look in the rearview mirror to confirm that the state trooper was still tailing us. She also reached to turn up the volume on the radio and then slumped in her seat a little bit, trying to relax.

Although my moms was trying to play shit cool, the truth was, I knew that she was just as nervous as I was.

"Ma, I already switched lanes, I gotta get off now or we'll look too suspicious," I explained over the loud R. Kelly and Snoop Dogg song that was coming from the speakers.

As soon as I switched lanes and attempted to make my way to the ramp of exit 13, the state trooper threw on his lights, signaling for me to pull over.

"Ain't this a bitch. Chyna, I told yo' ass."

"Ma, just chill," I barked, cutting my mother off. I was panicking and trying to think fast, and the last thing I needed was for my mother to be bitchin' with me.

"I got this. I'ma pull over and talk us outta this. Just follow my lead," I said with my heart pounding as I exited the parkway ramp and made my way on to

Linden Boulevard before bringing the car to a complete stop.

I had my foot on the brake and both of my hands on the steering wheel. I inhaled and then exhaled very deeply before putting the car in park. I quickly exited the car, wearing my Cartier Aviator gold-rimmed shades to help mask my face. The loud R. Kelly chorus continued playing in the background.

"Officer, I'm sorry if I was speeding, but—"

"Miss, step away from the car and put your hands where I can see them," the lone state trooper shouted at me, interrupting my words. He was clutching his nine-millimeter handgun, that was still in its holster, and he cautiously approached me. Soon, I no longer heard the music coming from the car and I was guessing that my mother had turned it down so that she could try to listen to what the officer was saying.

"Put my hands on the car for what? Let me just explain where I'm going."

The officer wasn't trying to hear it, and he slammed me up against the hood of the car.

"I got a sick baby in the car. What the hell is wrong with you?" I screamed. I was purposely trying to be dramatic while squirming my body and resisting the officer's efforts to pat me down.

On the inside I was still shitting bricks and my

heart was still racing a mile a minute. The car was in park at the side of the road and the engine was running idle. I was hoping that my mom would jump into the driver's seat and speed the hell off. There was no sense in both of us getting bagged. And from the looks of things, the aggressive officer didn't seem like he was in the mood for bullshit.

"Is anyone else in the car with you?" the cop asked me as he felt between my legs up to my crotch, checking for a weapon, even though he was clearly feeling for more than just a weapon.

My mother's BMW 745 that I was driving had limousine-style tints, and the state trooper couldn't fully see inside the car.

"Just my moms and my sick baby. Yo, on the real, for real, this is crazy. I ain't even do shit and you got me bent over and slammed up against the hood of the car feeling all on my pussy and shit! I got a sick baby that I'm trying to get to the hospital," I yelled while trying to fast-talk the cop. I sucked my teeth and gave him a bunch of eye-rolling and neck-twisting ghetto attitude.

"You didn't do shit? Well, if this is a BMW, then tell me why the fuck your plates are registered to a Honda Accord," the six-foot-four-inch drill-sergeant-looking officer screamed back at me.

The cop then reached to open up the driver's door, and just as he pulled the car door open, my moms opened her passenger door. She hadn't taken off the shades or the hat that she had been wearing, and with one foot on the ground and her other foot still inside the car she stood up and asked across the roof of the car if there was a problem.

"Chyna, you okay? What the fuck is going on, Officer?" my mother asked, sounding as if she was highly annoyed.

"Miss, I need you to step away from the car," the officer shouted at my mother.

"Step away from the car for what?" my moms yelled back with even more disgust in her voice.

"Ma, he on some bullshit. I told him that Nina is in the backseat sick as a damn dog and he still on this ol' racist profiling shit."

As soon as I was done saying those words I heard gunfire erupting.

Blaow. Blaow. Blaow. Blaow.

Instinctively I ducked for cover down near the wheel well, next to the car's twenty-two-inch chrome rims. And when I turned and attempted to see where the shots were coming from all I saw was the state trooper dropping to the ground. I turned and looked the other way and saw my mom's arms stretched across the roof of the BMW. She was holding her chrome thirty-eight revolver with both hands, ready to squeeze off some more rounds.

"Chyna, you aight?"

"Yeah, I'm good," I shouted back while still half-way crouched down near the tire.

"Well, get your ass in this car and let's bounce!" my moms screamed at me.

I got up off the ground from my kneeling stance and with my high-heeled Bottega Veneta boots I stepped over the bloody state trooper, who wasn't moving. He had been shot point-blank right between the eyes and he didn't look like he was breathing all that well, as blood spilled out of the side of his mouth.

Before I could fully get my ass planted on the cream-colored plush leather driver's seat my mom was hollering for me to hurry up and pull off.

"Drive this bitch, Chyna! I just shot a fucking cop! Drive!"

My mom's frantic yelling had scared my ten-month-old baby, who was strapped in her car seat in the back. So with my moms screaming for me to hurry up and drive away from the crime scene and with my startled baby crying and hitting high notes

I put the car in drive and I screeched off, leaving the cop lying dead in the street.

If shit wasn't thick enough for me and my mom already, killing a state trooper had definitely just made things a whole lot thicker. I sped off doing about sixty miles an hour down a quiet residential street in Elmont, Long Island, just off of Linden Boulevard. My heart was thumping and although it was late afternoon on a bright and sunny summer weekday, I was desperately hoping that no eyewitnesses had seen what went down.

2

**Rewind Back:
The History**
June 30, 2006
Harlem, New York

It was about eight thirty at night when my mother walked through the door, screaming out my name. She was hollering for me to come downstairs and meet Panama Pete. The infamous Panama Pete.

"Chyna, we back. Come downstairs and speak to Panama."

I had just laid my daughter down in her crib and I was trying to get some sleep before heading to the club later that night, but I knew that I couldn't be disrespectful. I got up outta my bed, threw on some Daisy Duke shorts and a white wife beater and slippers, and headed downstairs.

"Hey, Panama," I said with the phoniest smile

that I could muster up. I had spoken to Panama on a number of occasions when he had called from prison to speak to my mom, but I had never gone with her on any trips to visit him while he was locked up. So this was literally my first time ever meeting him.

"Waaowww!" Panama said after I had reached up on my tippy-toes and given him a kiss on the cheek. He held on to both of my hands while taking two steps back to look at me more closely.

"The last time I saw you, you was like two or three years old, running around with a diaper and a pacifier in your mouth."

I blushed as I looked at Panama. From all the pictures I had seen of him, I knew that he was a good-looking dude, but now that I was seeing him face-to-face I could honestly say that all the pictures I had seen him in hadn't done him any justice. In person he looked like the spitting sexy-ass image of the actor Tyrese Gibson, only he was taller than Tyrese Gibson and he had about forty pounds more muscle than Tyrese Gibson.

"God damn! I can't believe how good you look. You a grown-ass woman now," Panama added with extra emphasis.

"She look just like me, don't she?" my mom spoke up and asked, sounding all proud and shit.

"Yeah, but Roxy, when you was like seventeen, eighteen, you ain't look that damn good and have all that body," Panama joked.

"Nigga, fuck you. You know I always kept it thorough. And I still keeps it thorough for thirty-two years old," my mom replied. And she wasn't lying. My mother looked a lot like the actress LisaRaye. She was just as pretty as LisaRaye, with the same light complexion and long hair, only she was much more voluptuous, especially in the ass and hips. As for me, I was only eighteen years old and I was the spitting image of my mother, only I had more of a honey-coated complexion, similar to Beyonce's. Like my mother, I was thick in the ass, but where we differed was in the breasts—I had nice, full 36D breasts, compared to my mother's firm 34Cs.

I walked over to the TV and turned on BET to watch music videos and I told Panama that it was probably the McDonald's and the Wendy's that I be eating which made me so thick in all the right places.

"You know they got steroids or something up in that meat. Look at these video chicks—some of them is younger than me, with bodies like thirty-year-old women. I'm telling you, it comes from that Burger King and shit," I said with all seriousness.

"Roxy, a nigga is home. I'm free. I'm back! What!" Panama screamed.

After Panama said that, my mother walked into the kitchen to get a bottle of champagne and a bottle of Hennessy.

"We gotta pop these bottles," my mother shouted.

I knew that there was a bunch of other people in the house who had been chilling downstairs in the living room and in the basement throughout the day, waiting to surprise Panama and welcome him home, so I played everything cool and just made small talk with Panama.

"So did my mother tell you about tonight?" I asked.

"Oh, no doubt. It's on fo'sho tonight," Panama said.

"You know I dance at the spot we going to, right?"

"Word? Nah, I ain't know that," Panama said as he nodded his head and looked at me lustfully. "So that's what you do? You ain't got no man holding you down?" he asked as his hand found its way to my thigh. We were both sitting on the plush living room sofa watching the forty-two-inch flat screen.

"Yeah, that's what I do. So I'll make sure that

you have a good time tonight," I said as I removed Panama's hand from my thigh. I mean, I knew the nigga had just done fifteen years and hadn't had no pussy since George Bush's father was the president, but goddamn the nigga was moving way too fast.

At that point my mother returned to the living room with the champagne and the Hennessy, and she was accompanied by a whole host of other niggas and chicks who had run and hid in the kitchen when they heard my mother and Panama coming through the door.

"What up, my nigga?" one of Panama's homeboys said as he rushed him and gave him a ghetto embrace that sent both of them falling to the ground like they were playing tackle football or some shit.

"Ohhhh, shit. What the fuck? What up?" Panama shouted back. He was obviously happy as hell to see all the surprise guests.

"Chyna, go get me some cups and throw on some music and get those chicken wings and bring them out here," my mother whispered to me as one by one everyone greeted and embraced Panama Pete and welcomed him home.

I poured myself some Hennessy on the rocks and then I put a DJ Clue mix tape on and turned the volume on full blast before also cracking open the Ace of Spades.

I went to the kitchen and placed the chicken wings in the microwave, and as they warmed up I got a bunch of cups and some ice and some more liquor. Then I headed back to the living room so that I could be a good hostess and serve everybody as they mingled and reminisced with Panama Pete.

Actually, it was my honor to pour drinks and fix plates of food for everybody simply because the group of niggas and bitches that were in my living room had all been either directly down with or affiliated with the legendary CSC: the Chris Styles Crew.

Back in the mid to late eighties all the way through the early nineties, the Chris Styles Crew, which was started and headed by a Harlem-born hustler named Chris Styles, ran New York and most of the East Coast. In New York in particular, CSC had all of Harlem and all of the South Bronx on smash when it came to narcotics distribution. CSC was also responsible for supplying large parts of Baltimore, Washington, D.C., and Norfolk, Virginia, with drugs during the violent and profitable crack cocaine era.

Chris Styles, who is doing double life in Marion,

Illinois, in the same supermax federal penitentiary that housed John Gotti, was of course the number one man in CSC. But Panama Pete, who had just finished his bid at the Loretto Federal Correctional Institution, was the number two man in the CSC organization.

So, needless to say, everybody who was in the living room was there out of respect for Panama Pete. In fact, to not be there would have kind of been like a slap in the face, or going against the code of the street. In that living room there were about fifteen dudes and six chicks, and between them all they had done more than one hundred years in prison. I would also estimate that in that room were people who had been responsible for five hundred to one thousand murders, if not more. And also in that room were people who had helped to build and run a street organization that had done like a hundred million dollars in business throughout the years.

There were chicks like Puddin', Peaches, Shanice, and Lady Linda, and guys like Cisco, Ci-Lo, Reggie Rock, Dunkin' Hines, P.J., Bless, and Knowledge. All true hustlers, gangstas, and ballers in every sense of the word.

My mother, Roxy Reynolds, was also a part of

CSC, as was my deceased father, who I had never known. He was half-Jamaican and half-Chinese, which is how I got my name, Chyna. My father was also high in rank in CSC. Although he was only four years younger than Panama Pete, he was still number three in the organization, right behind Panama Pete. But he had been killed while my mother was still carrying me in her womb, so we never had a life together.

My mom had been down with CSC since she was thirteen years old. In fact, by the time I was five years old and my mom was just the tender age of nineteen, she had seen all that the streets had to offer, and she had done it all. She did everything from packaging drugs to running drugs to other states to selling drugs hand-to-hand to petty prostitution, and she'd even participated in her share of drive-bys and beat downs of rivals. Street life was all my mother had ever known. She literally never worked a legitimate job for one second of her life.

Like mother, like daughter; I was following in her footsteps. I, too, had never worked a legitimate nine-to-five job in my life, I had a small baby daughter out of wedlock, and I was addicted to fast money. And like my mother, I, remarkably, had never been convicted of any felonies. We had been arrested on numerous occasions but never convicted. Thank God my mother had never copped out to any charges, and she had never blew trial on the two occasions her cases went to trial.

The thing was, my mom was smart as hell. She understood the streets, and she had been mentored by and ran with the best. And all that she had learned over the years she was now passing on to me. As a mother-daughter team we weren't doing too bad. We had a nice-ass brownstone that we owned and lived in in Harlem. My mom had a BMW 745, and I had the Mercedes-Benz truck.

By night I hustled as a stripper in a spot called A Taste of Chocolate, which was also located in Harlem. And by day I helped my mother successfully operate a gunrunning ring that she'd started and headed, which we dubbed Harlem Heat.

Our Harlem Heat gunrunning operation kept food in my daughter's mouth, it kept all of the bills paid, and it kept me and my moms fly to death in all the latest shit. It allowed us to take exotic trips, and to floss in all of the clubs, and to trick money on niggas as if we were record company executives.

Me and my mother had the perfect dynamics for

making money, but the main reason that me and my mom clicked was because I learned from an early age not to ask questions and not to tell shit and just to deny the realities of what I was witnessing.

When I was twelve years old, I started to realize that my mother was a hustler and that she got her money however she had to get it. I remember as clear as day the first time a shitload of cops showed up at our house in the middle of the night with a search warrant and began kicking in the front door. I remember that night not because of the terrifying noise that the police made when they were breaking down the door, but because my mother had run into my bedroom half-naked and frantic and panicked. She had yanked me out of my bed and flipped over my mattress and grabbed what at the time looked to me like a clear thick plastic bag of flour. And she ran off to the bathroom with it.

"Mommy, what's the matter?" I asked as my heart pumped with fear from being startled and woken up so quickly.

"Chyna, everything is okay. Just go back in your room!" my mother screamed at me as she ripped the bag open and began pouring its contents into the toilet bowl.

I stood there frozen and watching my mother's every move.

"Chyna, go to your fucking room, I said!" my mother yelled at me as she flushed the toilet.

As I ran to my room I was greeted by gun-toting, bulletproof vest-wearing police officers who grabbed me and raced downstairs with me. It was like a scene from a movie, and things happened so fast that I didn't have time to get scared.

"Y'all better get the fuck outta my house!" my mother screamed at the cops. "I swear to God y'all better have a fucking warrant."

The cops sat me down on the living room couch and as I cleaned the cold outta my eyes they brought my mother downstairs in handcuffs and sat her down next to me. They showed her the search warrant and told her to shut the fuck up before they placed her under arrest.

"Arrest me for what? Y'all running up in my crib, scaring my daughter half to death, and you want me to be quiet? Y'all must be fucking crazy."

Like a little baby cub sitting next to its mother I felt safe, and although I didn't know what the hell was going on, I trusted that since I was with my mother that everything would be okay. And as we sat on the couch the cops ransacked our house. They turned over chairs and threw clothes outta closets and drawers and moved furniture. But after thirty minutes or so I remember them taking the handcuffs off of my mother and leaving just as fast as they had come.

"Chyna, you see this shit? You see what they did to this house? I can't stand those motherfucking pigs! Cops is always accusing me of shit for no reason," my mother explained to me as she surveyed the mess the cops had created.

"Why did they come here?" I asked as I followed behind my mother. "What were they looking for?"

"They came here 'cause they always fucking with me, that's why."

There was a pause in my mother's words as she went for the phone. Before she dialed she looked at me and sternly told me not to mention to anybody what had happened with the cops.

"Chyna, you didn't see nothing and you don't know nothing. If *anybody* asks you anything about what goes on in this house you tell they ass to speak to me. You understand me?"

I nodded my head and told my mother that I did understand her. And it seemed like from that moment on I knew to never snitch on my mother, and my don't-ask-don't-tell mentality and my state of denial about my mother's hustling ways began to kick in. And I fully bought into her continued assertion that she was just a faultless victim of overzealous and jealous cops who constantly chose to pick on her and single her out for no reason. My mentality was similar to that of a mafia wife who doesn't say shit but fully knows what her husband is into—to her, her husband can do no wrong, and it's everyone else just giving him a bad rap.

I held on to and cemented that mentality and as I grew older it only grew stronger. Call it brainwashing or whatever you wanna call it, but it became a part of who I was at the core. What was wild was that things never changed. If anything, they got worse as the government and the police, through arrests and convictions and snitches, managed to dry up all of the CSC money and straight humble niggas and chicks who, in their day, used to be holding some serious paper. In fact, my mom was like one of the only ones left from CSC who was still really getting money.

She was still getting money because she was smart and she adapted to the times. She knew that the whole drug era had passed and moved on and was totally saturated with niggas going for self. That whole concept of a crew controlling shit was long gone. According to my mother, she viewed the niggas from today's generation as stupid. See, she theorized that if niggas wasn't so selfish and solely focused on getting their own work so they could hustle for themselves, and more focused on aligning with a powerful crew that controlled shit, it would be a lot better for everybody.

"Chyna, everybody can eat and eat a whole lot better if they went off the same model that people like Chris Styles implemented back in the eighties," my mother explained to me one of the numerous times she schooled me on street life. "See, back in the day, you had cats like Chris Styles who would be caking off crazy and really making serious dough. But nobody was jealous because if Chris was making money that meant that the whole crew was making money and everybody had theirs. But now niggas would rather nobody have anything if they can't be the man on top controlling shit, and that mentality is why the street money is so fucked up."

I knew exactly where my moms was coming from because it was no different than the strip-club world. I danced at A Taste of Chocolate, and since it was the hottest strip club in New York it was always packed and by default I would make money. I didn't have to own the strip club to cake off from it; all I had to do was play my position and be a part of the movement.

Soon after I had served everyone their chicken and liquor the room became increasingly loud with talk and chatter, and it got more crowded, as more and more people kept arriving at the house to welcome Panama home.

All the noise inside the house woke my daughter up. I was surprised that I even heard her crying over all the loud music and the talking, but I went upstairs to get her and brought her back downstairs to meet and mingle with everybody.

My daughter was wearing just a diaper and she was sucking on her pacifier and looking around wide-eyed at all the faces that were crammed into the living room. Although Nina couldn't talk or really understand anything that was going on, just having her in the presence of all the hustlers in the room was similar to the way that my mother had indoctrinated me into that whole fast-money lifestyle.

"Nina, say hello to Uncle Panama," I said to my daughter.

"This is your baby? How old is she?" Panama said as he took the pacifier out of Nina's mouth. Nina gave him a look like she was ready to kill.

"Oh, shit. I see she just like her grandmother. She don't take no shit," Panama said as he placed the pacifier back into Nina's mouth.

My mother then turned down the music and spoke up.

"I wanna get everybody's attention," my mother shouted, and then she paused and waited for everybody to get quiet. "I need everybody to get a drink in their hands so we can toast Panama and officially welcome him home."

Everybody scrambled to get a drink, and when all the drinks were in place my mom continued.

"We got a lot of generations in this room. I know I'm a grandmother, but don't get it twisted—I'm only thirty-two years old and still sexy as a motherfucka," my mom said and everyone laughed. "But all jokes aside, I wanna toast this man right over here, this big sexy-ass bald-headed nigga right here. Panama Pete, my baby. He's a man's man. Everybody might not know this, but my daughter was only three years old when he went in the joint. Now she's all grown up with a daughter of her own, so it's like while Panama did his time, whole new generations was developing and shit. And you know what? In his near forty years on this earth Panama ain't never shed no tears, he ain't never roll over and snitch on nobody to make it better on himself, nah, none of that shit. He did his time like a man. And we need to respect his history and respect him for who he is and honor this motherfucka right here. So now I need everybody to raise they cups up and touch the person's cup next to yours as we toast to arguably one of the best to ever do it big on these Harlem streets. Give it up, everybody!" my mother said as she touched my cup with her cup and then took a swig of her champagne. Then she went and kissed Panama on the cheek.

"Oh, yo, one more thing. I know y'all all heard the DJs on the radio all week long, blowing up Panama's welcome-home party tonight at the club. So at eleven o'clock we heading over to A Taste of Chocolate, and we gonna keep this welcome-home celebration rocking all night long. So when we leave here I don't want nobody going home; I want all of us rolling up in there real deep at the same time," my mother shouted. She then instructed me to turn the music back up and I threw on Tony Yayo's hit record "So Seductive."

"Chyna, come here for a second," my mother hollered over to me as the music blasted in the background.

I came toward my mother and she asked me if I was working at the club that night, and if so what time I was heading to A Taste of Chocolate, and who I was gonna get to watch the baby. After I answered her she handed me an envelope.

"Twelve is too late. Listen, I need you to get there at like ten-thirty. There's two thousand dollars in that envelope. Take care of whoever you gotta take care of, but I don't want Panama paying for shit. I want them bringing him bottle after bottle and treating that nigga like a fucking king. Aight?"

"Okay. No doubt. I got it."

"And Chyna, I want two chicks giving him some ass at the same time, three chicks if you can swing it. Don't have no frontin'-ass chicks grinding up on him unless they gonna fuck."

"Ma, this is what I do! We gonna hold him down. I got this. Don't worry."

I headed upstairs and got my daughter ready for the babysitter. I had to hurry up because I also had to take a shower and get dressed. I knew that I had a long night ahead of me. But I also knew that it was gonna be a fun night and that I was gonna make a hell of a lot of money at the club.

The only thing that I was worried about was whether my baby's father was gonna show up at the club or not. I had never told my mother, but my baby's father, whose name is Lorenzo—he's much older than me, thirty to be exact—who's from Queens, had never met Panama Pete, but he hated the ground that he walked on because he swore to no end that Panama Pete was a snitch straight up and down.

Lorenzo insisted that although Panama Pete may have never ratted out anybody from CSC, he secretly dry-snitched on his rivals on a number of different occasions after he'd gone to prison, and that was the only reason that one of the counts he'd been convicted on was miraculously thrown out later. According to Lorenzo, Panama didn't just have better luck than his boss Chris Styles, who'd gotten a double life sentence; nah, he'd received preferential treatment because he was a *cooperator*.

To Lorenzo it just wasn't right for Panama to be walking around free and shit while the niggas he ratted on were doing football numbers in prison. Especially if one of those niggas Panama had ratted on was one of Lorenzo's boys.

Out of respect for me and my moms, Lorenzo had given me his word that he would let shit rest when Panama came home. But I knew that now that Panama Pete was in fact finally home, it would be really hard for Lorenzo to honor his word.

Although Lorenzo insisted to me that Panama Pete had been a confidential informant for the Feds and that I needed to watch that nigga closely, I had given him my word that I wouldn't say anything to my moms about the specifics of what he told me. I just hoped that nothing jumped off with Panama. Because if it did, and if Lorenzo was behind it, my moms would probably murder me for not having hipped her to what was up. But hey, that was just the type of risk that I dealt with every day. It was part of the fast life that I lived. It was the only life I'd ever known.

3

Ghetto Celebrity

By the time my mom, Panama Pete, and their whole entourage arrived at the strip club it was well past midnight and the club was filled to capacity. I made sure that the manager had reserved a section in the VIP area for my mom and her crew. So when they arrived I quickly took three other dancers with me and we made our way over to where my mom was.

"Shout out to my man Panama Pete, who just walked in the house! Welcome home from Loretto. I see you, Baby Pa. Ladies, make sure y'all show him some love," DJ John Blaze shouted into the microphone.

As soon as I was face-to-face with Panama he

became touchy-feely and started grabbing on my ass, which was in an enticing G-string. I knew that he was drunk so I didn't trip over it.

"Panama, these are my girls, I wanted to introduce them to you," I shouted into Panama's ear over the loud music.

"Hello, ladies," Panama replied. "Y'all looking good."

I looked over at my mother and she smiled and nodded her head to show her approval of the chicks I had chosen for Panama. My Puerto Rican girl Cathy had on a pink G-string bottom and a matching top and white stilettos. My other, light-skinned homegirl, Candy, had on an all-white slingshot-style bikini and clear stilettos. And my dark-skinned homey named Camry had on thigh-high zebra-print stockings with a matching bra and thong, along with black heels.

"They gotchu for the whole night," I reached up and whispered into Panama's ear. "*Whatever* you want."

Panama smiled and nodded, and then went to sit down. Candy and Camry both followed him and sat on his lap while Cathy stood in front of him and danced by herself to the music that was playing.

Before long, bottle after bottle was being popped open and the liquor was freely flowing.

"Panama, we gonna take it back to the eighties for you, my nigga. Then we gonna switch it up and take it to the early nineties. Come on!" the DJ shouted as he threw on the old-school smash-hit record by Rakim, "Eric B. Is President."

Everybody went crazy when that song came on and the place was rocking as if it was a regular dance nightclub and not a strip club.

"Easy, Camry, be easy. There's a lot of under-covers up in here. Shout out to all the Feds and the plainclothes cops in the house!" John Blaze shouted, laughing into the microphone. He then switched up the music and started playing "Gin and Juice," saying, "I told y'all we was going to the early nineties. Let's go!"

Camry was kissing on Panama's neck and rubbing on his chest while Candy and Cathy switched places. At that point Candy was dancing in front of Panama while Cathy sat on his lap, grinding her ass on him.

The DJ then threw on another one of Snoop Dogg's hit records from the *Deep Cover* sound track. "This is for all the po-po in the fucking house. *It's 187 on a motherfuckin' cop!*" he shouted along with the lyrics of the song.

In no time the entire VIP area was crammed

to capacity with music-industry celebrities and everyday niggas who were practically lining up to suck Panama's dick. One by one people showed him love and paid homage to him, and he soaked up every minute of the attention like the true ghetto celebrity that he was.

"Your name Chyna?" some dude that I had never seen before asked me.

"Yeah, that's me."

"Yo, how much for a private dance?" the guy asked me.

"Thirty dollars a song," I quickly replied, trying hard to figure out how the dude knew my name.

Then I looked and saw this other dude with a wad of money in his hands. He was peeling off twenty-dollar bills as if they were singles and dropping them in front of Candy for her to pick up. He was clearly trying to chump Panama. So of course one of Panama's boys stepped to the dude to check his ass.

"Aight, come on, sweetie. I'm ready for this dance," the dude who had asked if my name was Chyna said to me as he placed a hundred-dollar bill into my hand.

"Hold up a minute," I replied and handed the money back to him. I could sense that something was about to jump off with Panama, and Panama was my mother's people, which by default made him my people. So if something jumped off I would have to be there to help out.

"Chyna, come here. Stay close to me," the dude said to me as he grabbed me.

"Yo, get the fuck off of me! I can't give you that dance right now!" I barked at the persistent dude who was quickly becoming a pain in the ass.

He grabbed hold of me again and said, "Lorenzo told me to keep you close to me. Shit is about to go down."

I looked at the dude and then glanced back over to where my mother was. I saw Panama get to his feet, along with my mother and like six other people from her crew. They were beefing and they had that look like they were ready for war. Then the next thing I knew I saw champagne and beer bottles flying and fist and feet swinging, and an all-out brawl ensued.

"Shorty, come on!" the dude said to me as he scooped me off my feet and ran with me to the other side of the club.

Bang bang bang bang bang.

That's the sound that I heard through the loud music, and I knew that they were definitely gunshots.

I kept screaming for the dude to let me go but he was way stronger than I was and he wouldn't loosen his grip. Everyone who had rushed over to the VIP area to see what was going on quickly changed direction, and there was a stampede for the exit doors once people heard the gunshots. It was a straight melee and a zoo inside the club. The lights came on and the music was turned off and there was this loud screeching sound that was caused by the feedback from a microphone that had been dropped too close to a speaker.

Finally I freed myself from the guy's grip and ran over to the VIP area, toward the gunshots. I saw liquor spilled everywhere, I saw tables and chairs turned over, and I saw one dude laid out cold on the floor. I looked and saw a few people bleeding as I desperately scanned the club looking for my mother, but I couldn't locate her or Panama. So I immediately ran back to the dressing room to my locker and got my cell phone and dialed my mother's cell.

"Ma, you okay?" I screamed into the phone as soon as my mother answered.

"Yeah, yeah, we good. We outside, headed to the car. We ain't trying to stay up in there with all them cops and shit walking around."

"What the fuck happened?" I asked.

"It's nothing. Just jealous, hating-ass mother-fuckers!"

"I saw a dude dropping money in front of Candy while she was dancing for Panama, and then the next thing I know motherfuckas was fighting," I said.

"That's what I'm saying. It's them jealous, hating niggas. Some dude blew smoke in Panama's face. Now you know, is he stupid or what? Like, does he know who the hell he's fucking wit'?"

"Say word?" I said to my mother, since I hadn't seen that part go down.

"Word. But listen, I want you to find out exactly who that was. Just ask around. 'Cause whoever it is, we gots to bring it to 'em."

"Aight, definitely," I replied.

"Chyna, hurry up and get your ass up outta that spot. We heading to the crib. I'll see you when you get in," my mother said as she hung up.

As I changed out of my G-string and stilettos and prepared to go home I couldn't help but shake my head as I thought about how Panama Pete had just finished a fifteen-year bid and hadn't been home for more than a full twelve hours and yet there was drama with his ass already. From that moment I knew that having Panama around was gonna be nothing but trouble for me and my mom.

4

A Gangsta's Pride

Before I could get fully dressed, there were cops and news crews everywhere. The cops weren't trying to let anybody leave the club because they were searching everyone for weapons and drugs and they were trying to question as many people as they could. I was sure that it had to be an absolute zoo outside in front of the club.

Thankfully, forty-five minutes or so later, the cops finally let me go. But I hung around the club for about an hour and kicked it with some of the other dancers and one of the bartenders before leaving. By the time I left there were still cops and people milling around everywhere. When I finally did bounce from the club I decided I would leave my daughter at the babysitter's house and shoot straight to my crib to see what was up and to find out more details as to exactly what went down with the fight inside the club.

As I headed home, I was thinking about calling Lorenzo and using the whole Panama thing as an excuse to get him to let me and Nina stay with him. Although Lorenzo messed with other women, he definitely would have let me and Nina stay with him at any time and for any reason. But I never wanted to come at him through the *back door*. It was like I wanted him to *want* me and Nina to stay with him and live with him, and invite us through the front door.

See, I loved Lorenzo, and he was the only dude that I was letting sex me on a consistent basis, but for whatever reason he just wasn't feeling me the same way I was feeling him and he would never let himself get close to me emotionally. I think it was partly because of my age. I was young when I started messing with him and I think that because of my age he never really took me seriously, and just looked at me as a convenient piece of young pussy.

On the flip side, I always looked at Lorenzo as the ideal man that I wanted to be with, and I was stupid enough to think that having his baby would cause him to wanna wife me, which obviously didn't happen. So although we weren't a committed couple, we were bound to each other because of Nina, and in my mind I always hoped that we would eventually become a family.

I made it to my house on 135th Street expecting to see and be greeted by the same Chris Styles Crew members who had been at my house earlier, welcoming Panama home from prison. But to my surprise I didn't walk into a house full of niggas; instead I walked in on obnoxiously loud screams of ecstasy coming from my mother, who was in her room getting fucked by somebody.

"Take this pussy baby! Take that shit!" my mother screamed.

I shook my head as I walked near my mom's closed bedroom door and headed to my bedroom. I could hear the metal headboard of her bed rhythmically banging into the wall, and it sounded as if a carpenter were trying to put a hole in the wall with a sledgehammer or some shit.

"You like this dick?"

"Yeah, I like it," my mother shouted.

"This is my pussy?"

"Yes it's your pussy!"

"Say my mothafucking name!"

"Panama!" my mother shouted, sounding like some young naïve hood rat as opposed to the high-powered sexy chick she was.

When I heard that, my jaw almost dropped to the floor.

My mother was never quiet when it came to sex. She was a screamer, and she always let the neighbors in on what she was doing and how good it was based on how loud she hollered. So I was used to her being a screamer—that didn't shock me. But what had shocked the hell outta me was the fact that she was letting Panama fuck her.

I was surprised because I had always thought that her and Panama's relationship was more of a cool-ass brother-and-sister type of relationship. Plus, from everything that my mom had ever told me about my father, I knew Panama was his friend; she would almost always mention Panama's name in the same breath with any stories about my dad because of how close my dad and Panama had been.

I made my way to the bathroom and turned on the shower, which helped to drown out the sounds of their ghetto lovemaking session. I always took long, thirty-minute showers and made good use of my many different shower gels, my mesh sponge, and my loofah pad.

When my shower was over I made it to my room and started applying lotion and baby oil to my body. Apparently my mom and Panama had finished doing the deed and my mother walked up to my bedroom door and stood at the entrance to my room with her robe on and a blunt in her hand.

"What's up, girl?" she said to me as she turned her lips to the right side of her face and blew some weed smoke into the room. "Where's Nina?"

"She still at the babysitter's. I decided I'll just pick her up in the morning."

There was a brief silence on my mother's part, and then she stepped all the way into my room and closed the door behind her.

"Panama is gonna be staying with us for a while, until he can get his shit situated," my mother informed me with a lowered voice.

"Oh *really*?" I asked sarcastically. "Ma, we only got three fucking bedrooms and I ain't giving up mines, and I don't wanna move Nina into my bedroom, either."

"Chyna, don't you think I already fucking know

that? He's gonna sleep downstairs on the couch in the living room, so this way it's cool for everybody," my mom explained.

I continued applying lotion to my body and slowly shook my head. I wanted to say something to my mother about what Lorenzo had told me in terms of Panama being a snitch but I kept my mouth closed on that. But I couldn't hold my tongue when it came to my not being happy about her decision to let Panama crash with us.

"Ma, I got Nina up in here. If she wasn't here then you know I wouldn't trip about shit and everything would be all good. But with no disrespect to anybody, you seen the shit that went down tonight at the club. That drama was behind Panama. The nigga ain't been home a full day yet and cats is already coming for his neck, trying to test his ass, and I don't want that drama following him to our crib if my daughter is gonna be up in here."

My mother looked as if she was taking in my words; she also took another pull on her weed before speaking.

"Nina is my damn granddaughter. You think I would let something happen to her?"

I ain't say nothing because it didn't make sense

to respond. Whenever my mother's mind was made up about something she would rarely ever bend. So there was no sense in trying to make my point.

"So, Ma, what's up with you letting Panama hit it?"

"Chyna, you don't be questioning me about who I open my legs to! Who the fuck you think you dealing with?" my mother shouted at me with a twisted, screw-face look.

I sucked my teeth and responded with an attitude of my own. "All I'm saying is that ain't how you raised me. You raised me on that whole shit about respecting the game and all that, and here you are backing up on the same shit you been preaching."

"What the fuck you talking about?"

"I'm saying, Panama was daddy's homey. Right or wrong?"

"Right," my mom answered.

"So I'm saying, how the fuck you gonna let my father's right-hand man twist you out and not feel like that ain't disrespecting my father's name and his honor?"

"Girl, get off that bullshit. Your daddy been dead damn near nineteen fucking years! If he was alive then that would be different. But he ain't alive. There is no nigga *alive* who's gonna control what I do, and there damn sure ain't no way in hell that I'ma let a nigga control me from his grave!"

I simply rolled my eyes and didn't look in my mother's direction. I was hoping that she would just get the hell outta my room and go about her business so that I could go about mines. But she kept on talking, and she seemed as if she didn't have any plan to let up anytime soon.

"Besides, I only fucked the nigga to help him get his swagger back. The nigga just did fifteen years with no pussy, and now he's home and he ain't got shit."

"So that was a *pity* fuck?"

"Yeah, if you wanna call it that," my mom responded.

I shook my head but didn't say anything, but my moms had to know in her heart that she was breaking all the rules to the game that she had taught me. A damn pity fuck? I thought to myself. I couldn't believe it because it was always my mother who had told me and stressed to me to *never* fuck with pitiful niggas.

"Actually, though, it was more than that," she said quickly, in an effort to clean it up. "Chyna, these young cats don't respect the game no more, and they don't respect history. You seen them up in the club trying to chump Panama by dropping money in front of the chick that was dancing for him? What they was trying to say is Panama is powerless. He's a broke-ass nigga with history but no money, and money is power. And then on top of that to blow smoke in his face?"

"So that's why you fucked him? Still sounds like a *pity* fuck to me," I replied bluntly. "Just let the nigga handle his business like the man he's supposed to be."

My mother finally finished smoking her weed and then she continued explaining.

"Aight, Chyna, listen," she said while speaking in a whispered tone. "All niggas have pride, especially gangsta niggas like Panama. And I know that after tonight his pride and his ego is definitely gonna kick in, and when it does he's gonna start stressing and figuring out how he can make a quick come-up and get money and floss and all of that to show niggas that he's still the man."

I nodded my head in agreement. I'd finally finished putting lotion on my body.

"So I know he's gonna try to move in on what we built. *We,* meaning me and you. Chyna, we built

Harlem Heat. We took all the risks; we the ones running guns up and down I-95. And like I always told
you, there's risk and reward, and the reward gotta be
in proportion to the risks. Panama ain't take no risks
building this shit—we did. And I know he won't be
satisfied with just a piece of what we got going on.
He's gonna want the whole pie and try to leave us
with the scraps from what we fucking built."

I sat up because I was finally starting to see some
of the wisdom in my mother's sexual theatrics.

"So you're saying that you fucked the nigga to
let him think that there's love between you and him,
so this way when you gotta relegate his ass to soldier
status his ego won't be totally bruised."

"Exactly!" my moms replied. "I mean, don't get
me wrong, there's real genuine love for Panama. But
what I'm saying is that he can't just have this shit.
He can have a part of it, but not the whole thing,
and I know he's gonna want the whole thing. So it's
like I gotta do shit now that's gonna soften things
when I deliver that blow to him later. And like I said,
I got love for the nigga. Between me and you, quiet
as kept, not only did I fuck the nigga, I gave him five
G's tonight just so he could have some bread in his
hands. And that's on top of the two G's I gave you

earlier for his ass. So I'm going into my stash for the nigga, and my money is dipping real low right now, trust me. But I know how he looked out for me back in the day. And I can't forget that. I could have easily been doing twenty years and better had he ratted me out on that murder. I know that, and I'm extremely loyal. But even loyalty has its limits. You feel me?"

"No doubt I feel you," I said to my mom, as she had once again taught me a lesson, and at the same time she let me see even more just how smart she was.

I was with her a hundred percent. I didn't want Panama to try to take over what she and I had built, especially when I didn't know whether or not to believe my baby's father and his claims that Panama was a rat.

So my mother and I were on the same page in terms of Panama, and it was good that we were, just in case Panama tried to play me against my mother or vice versa. We also decided that since Panama's immediate family had turned their backs on him that we would hold him down for as long as we had to. If that meant him sleeping in our crib till he got on his feet, then we would do that. If it meant that we would finance him a whip until he got back on his feet, then we would do that, too. If it meant that we would steer him toward a hustle of his own, like pimping and prostitution, that he could control until he got on his feet, then we would do that. But we were both resolute on the fact that there was no way in hell that we were gonna just hand over control of Harlem Heat to Panama Pete. It just wasn't gonna happen.

Control of Harlem Heat—and particularly of the money it was bringing in—would be just what Panama Pete wanted. Unfortunately, though, a nigga can't always have what he wants, even if that nigga was the infamous street legend Panama Pete.

5

Blind Loyalty

Sure enough, about a month after Panama came home he started to put pressure on my mom to give him more control over Harlem Heat and to give him details on exactly who it was that was supplying her with the guns that we resold on the street.

My mom was no dummy, and being that she knew what Panama's game plan would be, she had already come up with excuses and ways to brush off his requests without him being too offended.

One of the things that she repeatedly told Panama, which was absolutely true, was that he was way too hot to be fucking around with any kind of major hustle, and that he needed to just lay low for about six months. Everyone with any kind of street smarts knew that the Feds would be constantly watching Panama from the moment he stepped foot outta jail. Just like it was no coincidence that the strip club was full of undercover cops on the night that Panama's welcome-home shindig got shot up. Those cops were there for one reason and one reason only—to conduct surveillance on Panama Pete.

In fact, when we found out exactly who it was who'd tried to punk Panama at the club that night, we decided not to retaliate because we knew that the cops had probably paid their informants to provoke the entire incident to begin with. So we just let it die for the time being.

"Ma, I know he's your homey and y'all got history and all of that, but on the real, you know and I know that dude is a fucking liability right now," I explained to my mom as we drove south on I-95, headed to Georgia to re-up on guns.

My mother looked at me but she didn't respond. She knew I was right, but it was like she was letting her heart overrule her head. I even started to question whether my mom had real feelings for Panama. I mean, she had completely depleted her stash for the nigga, and she had begun tapping into my stash just to support his ass and keep him fly.

She'd spent thirty thousand dollars buying him an all-black Yukon Denali truck. She'd bought him a pound of weed for his own personal use. She'd spent a couple of thousand on new gear for Panama. It was crazy. And it was the type of shit that a chick would only do for her man. Maybe I just didn't understand it because I wasn't cut from that old-school cloth, but to me it was stupid and I knew that no matter what my mother said it was just a matter of time before Panama Pete was gonna break her down and take over our hustle.

"Chyna, the nigga did build up a shitload of connections when he was in the joint, and we gonna get paid off those connections that he has," my moms explained.

She was referring to a bunch of criminal cats that Panama had met over the years in prison. He was promising to put us on to all these different cats so that we could supply them with guns.

"Ma, it's been a month and the nigga just been talking, but he ain't produce not one solid fucking connection yet! Meanwhile we going broke tricking all this dough on the motherfucker," I vented.

My mother was still letting Panama fuck her, and I knew that her feelings and emotions were starting to get wrapped up in the nigga, so I had to tread lightly and not come across too disrespectful.

"Chyna, I got this. Let me worry about Panama. Just trust me on this," my mother said.

I decided to drop it for the moment. I put in a DJ Whoo Kid mix tape and listened to that.

About an hour later my mom and I stopped at a Waffle House to get some food, and while we were eating I found I just couldn't hold my tongue anymore.

"Ma, listen, I'm just saying this on some real love shit, and I ain't trying to be disrespectful or nothing, but I just can't hold this shit back no more."

"What's up?" my mother asked as we sat in our booth and ate waffles, scrambled eggs, and bacon.

"I think that Panama is a fucking snitch," I said, and my heart rate picked up a little.

My mother looked at me and paused before putting a forkful of food in her mouth. Then she started laughing as if she were at a damn comedy club and asked me what the hell was I talking about.

"Lorenzo swears that the nigga is a snitch, and that's why he ain't been coming around to see Nina," I explained.

My mother shook her head, and then she let

loose on me. "Chyna, the first thing you need to understand is that Lorenzo ain't thinking about yo' ass. You constantly running behind the nigga, hoping he gonna wife you or something, but what you need to do is get off the nigga's dick 'cause he ain't about shit. He can't come by to see his goddamn daughter, probably 'cause he ain't holding no real money, so he gonna tell you some sideways shit like that about Panama. Lorenzo is from Queens, so what the hell does he know about anything concerning a Harlem nigga?"

My mother knew exactly how to get my blood pressure up. She knew that I really cared about Lorenzo, and whenever she wanted to piss me off she would push that button about Lorenzo not being about shit, and Lorenzo not caring about me. But I knew what I knew, and I know what I saw.

"Ma, I didn't believe Lorenzo at first, either, but I was at his crib in Queens and he showed me like three different discovery packages from niggas that's doing football numbers in prison and—"

"And what? Panama's name is listed in those discovery packages?" my mother cut me off.

"Not exactly, because they had him listed as a confidential informant, but in all of the different packages they alluded to him as a former high-ranking member of CSC."

My mother got up from the table and threw a twenty-dollar bill on the table.

"Chyna, I should jam this fork up your ass for saying that dumb shit. You better not repeat no shit like that to nobody. And tell Lorenzo and his bitch ass that just because he the father of my granddaughter that don't mean that his ass ain't above getting touched," my mother said, abruptly ending our breakfast before I was even finished.

When we got back into the car my mother would not let up about how vaguely listing characteristics of confidential informants in sworn affidavits was just a game that the Feds played in order to get motherfuckers talking and snaking each other. She swore that it was all bullshit that shouldn't be paid attention to, and then she went on and on for like thirty minutes straight about how there was no way that Panama could be a snitch and how he was a stand-up dude and how he could have rolled over on hundreds of niggas had he wanted to save his own ass—but he didn't.

"Chyna, keep your fucking mouth closed and don't mention this shit again to nobody, 'cause all you gonna do is stir up some unnecessary shit."

After that I basically kept my mouth closed for the remainder of the trip. We made it to Georgia about two hours after leaving that Waffle House and I was dead silent for the rest of the ride. Even when we met up with the white gun dealer I stayed in the car and let my mother handle the small transaction.

When we got to our hotel I did converse with my mother, in one-word yes and no responses, but it was clear that I had an attitude. My mother was basically showing blind loyalty to Panama. And blind loyalty was something that she had always schooled me against having.

She could be blind if she wanted to, but my eyes were gonna be wide open when it came to Panama Pete.

6

The Setup

By the middle of August I was more than tired of seeing and being around Panama. He was constantly keeping a shitload of disrespectful niggas around the house, at all hours of the day and night. I was tired of him coming out of the shower without a towel on. I was tired of him leaving the kitchen and bathroom dirty and not cleaning up after himself. I was tired of the nigga monopolizing the living room couch, smoking weed all the damn time. I was tired of the nigga dropping his clothes throughout the damn house. I was tired of the nigga blowing through money like it was water and then begging for more like a broke pitiful-ass nigga. And I was especially tired of the nigga disrespecting the crib

by bringing different chicken heads through to chill with him. The nigga was a definite liability, and he had to go or I was gonna go. There were no two ways
about it.

Financially my mother and I were going through a drought. We were making small gun runs, where we would make two thousand here, five thousand there, but the money we were making was being spent faster than it was coming in. I started secretly stashing most of the money that I was making from the strip club so that my moms wouldn't hit me up for it, and so I could have some kind of dough in case of an emergency.

What wasn't funny was the fact that Panama kept promising my mother this big home-run payday that she was gonna get from his connections, but he had yet to make good on it. And even though he hadn't made good on any of his connections, my mother was slippin' big time. She broke down the whole Harlem Heat operation to Panama. She told him which gun dealers we were buying our guns from and how we concealed them when we transported them. She taught him how to destroy the serial numbers on the guns. All of it. And even with all that information, Panama still never came through with

63

HARLEM HEAT

any of his so-called Italian Mafia connections, or his connections to white-boy skinheads he had came to know in prison.

Panama was all talk, and he appeared to me to just be some old has-been washed-up gangsta that had seriously lost his swagger. He was always talking about what he was gonna do when he made his come-up. Yet he wasn't getting off his ass to make it happen. And really, he didn't have to get off his ass and hustle; all he had to do was complain and feel sorry for himself about not having bread for this and bread for that or about sleeping on our couch and he knew that those sob stories were just gonna motivate my mother to look out for his ass, which is exactly what she kept doing.

But with Panama knowing our whole operation, I was scared as hell. I knew that my mother and I and some of our homegirls were gonna get locked up if Panama ever got bagged for anything because I knew that he would rat us out to save his ass.

The thing was, I knew that since Panama now knew exactly what we knew, and knew how our operation worked, as soon as he got his hands on some bread he was gonna go around us and start his own gunrunning ring. The only additional thing that he would need to go around us would be someone like me or my mother who had balls and who he could trust, and who also had no felony convictions. If he could find a person like that, someone who would be willing to get residency and a driver's license in Georgia, he would be able to duplicate what me and my mother had built. And I had a strong feeling that that was what he was planning, and that was why he had yet to produce any of his connections. He wanted to profit in full, on his own, from those connections.

Amid all the frustration I was feeling and with this drought that my mother and I were experiencing, I finally got a reason to smile: my mother had been in touch with this gangsta nigga from Newark, New Jersey, who was part of the Bloods street gang. The dude came to my moms wanting to buy a shitload of all kinds of high-powered machine guns, assault rifles, and handguns. It was like he was trying to arm a small army or some shit, but the thing was we didn't care what he wanted to use the guns for; all my moms and I cared about was if he could come up with the money for the transaction.

From the way my mother figured it, we stood to make about $50,000 in profit off of the transaction with the Bloods. She was gonna do what she always did: double the retail price of the guns and keep the extra money as our profit. But with a transaction that big my mother needed the dude to front $50,000 so that she could buy the guns, and then she would get the other $50,000 when the transaction was completed. Doing the deal that way reduced our risk.

"So you think you can trust this dude?" I asked my moms as we drove in her car to Carolines Comedy Club on Broadway.

"Yeah, I trust him. And Panama asked around about the dude and he checked out. So he's gonna roll with me to get the first half of that dough."

I slumped in my seat and shook my head and just turned up the volume on the radio. My mother was letting Panama get way too close, but I didn't say a word. I just went along with the flow.

About two weeks later, three days before Labor Day, my mother and Panama rolled out to Newark to pick up the $50,000. Everything went off without a hitch and they were able to get the money.

With the Labor Day holiday coming up, my mother didn't wanna rush and do the transaction too quickly and get tripped up by the police somehow. So she told the dude from the Bloods that she would have all his guns to him in a week's time, which meant the following Saturday, after Labor Day.

In the meantime, Panama wanted to celebrate and live it up but my moms decided to just chill and play things quiet. She didn't want anybody to even know about the deal except for me, her, and Panama.

Panama kept insisting that we at least go out to the 40/40 Club or somewhere like that and spend some of the money celebrating quietly among ourselves. I think the thing that Panama didn't understand was that back in the day, in the eighties and early nineties, $50,000 was a lot of dough. But fast-forward to 2006 and it was like $50,000 could easily be blown in a few days. It was a lot of money, but at the same time it wasn't that much money, relatively speaking.

What was funny was that Panama was definitely counting his chickens before they hatched. And he was being way too possessive, as if the money was *his* money, like he was the reason behind the deal with the Bloods.

"Roxy, this is about to be every day for us. I got these Italian cats from Howard Beach out in Queens, and they ready to fuck with us. I'm telling you, we gonna be doing two deals like this a month, easy!"

My mother didn't respond to Panama's enthusiasm with enthusiasm of her own. She just played along with whatever he said. All I hoped was that

my mother wouldn't give Panama more than $5,000 from the deal—and I thought even that was too much. But for the moment my mother wasn't divvying up anything. She stashed the money in a briefcase and placed the briefcase under her bed, where she knew it would be safe because no one had a key to her bedroom door, and she always kept her bedroom locked when she wasn't home. She didn't even give *me* a key to the room.

To calm Panama down, we decided to just go to the 40/40 Club and have a good time and pop some bottles. But as we started to get dressed and ready to go I just had to take a stab at Panama as I saw him walking to the bathroom.

"Panama, you ain't in the hole no more. We got showers and shit up in here, so can you please stop washing your dick in the fucking sink? I'm tired of cleaning up after your ass."

"What the fuck you say?" Panama asked me, stopping dead in his tracks and turning around to look at me. He was standing with just a white towel wrapped around his waist.

"You heard what the fuck I said."

Panama smirked and stared at me. I rolled my eyes at him and folded my arms across my chest and waited for him to say something.

"Yo, I'm gonna act like I didn't hear what you just said."

"No. I wantchu to act like you heard what I said. I said *stop washing your dick in the fucking sink*. You heard me now?" I screamed as I walked toward Panama to see what he was gonna do. I wanted him to hit me so I could call Lorenzo to come over and light his ass up and get him the hell outta our crib.

"Chyna, who are you yelling at like that?" my mother yelled from upstairs as she made her way down to the living room to see what was going on.

"Roxy, you need to come check your daughter."

"She ain't gotta come check me for shit. What you need to do is check your ass up outta this house and into a hotel so they can clean up after you," I shouted at Panama.

"Chyna!" my mother barked at me as she grabbed me by the shoulder. "What the hell is going on? I thought we was getting dressed to go to the club?"

"We are going, but I'm just telling the nigga to stop washing his dick in the damn sink. I'm tired of cleaning up after his ass and cleaning up his pubic hairs and all that ghetto nasty shit. He ain't in the hole no more, he's in a fucking house."

"Chyna, first of all, this is my goddamn house. Let's get that shit straight. And if you got a problem with Panama, you bring that shit to me."

"Nah, Roxy she ain't gotta bring nothing to you. She can bring it directly to me," Panama said, and he looked at me like he was ready to slap earth, wind, and fire outta me.

"Aight, I'll bring it to you, then. Yo' ass is sorry, broke, and pitiful. You always promising big money shit, but you ain't never delivering on what the fuck you say you gonna do. Then you just wanna spend our money like you balling? And now I ask you to stop washing your dick in the sink and you got a problem with that? Nigga, please," I said, and then I walked off and up to my room. At that point I no longer felt like going to the club.

"Roxy, if that wasn't your daughter I would have to choke her ass up for talking to me like that," Panama said to my mother, but loud enough for me to hear.

"Just chill and get ready to go. I'll talk to her."

My mother eventually did come up to my room, and she spoke to me and calmed me down and convinced me to just get dressed and go out with them to the club. I did eventually get dressed, and I went out with her and Panama, but for the entire night Panama and I were as cold as ice toward each other. We didn't speak to each other and we tried our best to not look in each other's direction. But he did the best job in the world at continuing to piss me off by spending money and flossing in the club like he was a true shot-caller, which he clearly no longer was. I wanted to walk up to him and tell him that he wasn't Jay-Z, so he needed to go and sit his ass down somewhere.

After that night at the 40/40 Club we waited for the week to pass us by so that we could complete the gun deal with the Bloods. But I knew that even with the money we were gonna make off of the deal I couldn't be lazy and that I had to keep making money from stripping and stashing it. I also knew that the Sunday before Labor Day would be a big-money night at the strip club because everybody would be off of work the following day.

And sure enough, I was right. That Sunday night I made all kinds of money. The club was packed to the brim with ballers who were spending money freely. And although I didn't count my money before leaving the club that night I knew that I had to have made about $2,000, if not more. But I also had worked my ass off for that money and by three-thirty in the morning I was beyond tired so I headed home to get some much-needed sleep.

When I reached home there were no parking spaces to be found on 135th Street so I circled the block a couple of times, but still found no spaces. I ended up parking about five blocks away and briskly walking to my house, my high heels *click-clacking* the whole way.

As soon as I set foot on the steps that led to my front door I heard somebody call out my name.

"Yo, Chyna."

I turned around but didn't see anybody.

"Chyna, that's you?" the male voice shouted again.

"Yeah, who dat?" I responded, since I still didn't see anybody.

Then from out of nowhere this dude dressed in all black and with a black bandanna tied around his face jumped out from behind a parked car, his gun pointed at me.

"Bitch, don't move, and don't fucking scream."

Immediately my heart started pounding and my

first instinct was to run and see if I could make it into my house, so I took off up the steps, frantically hoping I would make it to my door and up to my room and to get hold of my gun. I had always feared that some horny dude would follow me home from the club and try to rape me, and at that moment I just knew that my fears were about to become a living nightmare.

"Bitch, I said don't fucking move," the guy barked at me as he grabbed me from behind by my hair and yanked me down the concrete steps.

"Ah, shit!" I screamed out, wincing in pain. And even though the guy had a gun pointed at me I immediately went into fight mode. I was trying to get to my feet, and at the same time I was swinging my fists as fast as I could, but I knew that I was having little effect.

Whack.

The guy hit me upside the head with the butt of his gun and I immediately felt a stinging sensation run down the whole right side of my body, I felt like I was gonna pass out. I literally saw stars from the blow.

With the barrel of the gun stuffed in my mouth and me lying on the sidewalk of the deserted Harlem street the gunman leaned over and spoke in a grimy and raspy voice. "Say one more motherfucking word and you'll be leaking all over this fucking sidewalk."

I was scared as shit so I just nodded my head to show my surrender.

Then I saw the guy signaling with his left hand, as if he was waving to somebody to come to him.

And before I could blink, two other dudes, also dressed in black and with bandannas masking their faces, came from across the street. I heard a car door slam, and a car driving off, so I assumed that the two new thugs had just gotten out of that car.

"This how the fuck we gonna do this. Chyna, you gonna get up, walk up these steps, and let us in the crib, and you gonna keep your fucking mouth closed. Aight? If you scream, I'll murder you," the guy said as he cocked the gun in my mouth. From my experience with street life, and from the sound of the dude's voice, he definitely sounded credible and capable of following through on his threats.

"Hmm emh," I said, nodding with my eyes wide open and bulging out of the sockets. I was praying that his finger didn't pull that trigger by accident.

The dude pulled me to my feet and asked me who was in the house.

"My daughter and my moms," I replied nervously.

"Who the fuck else? And if you lying to me I'll fucking toss your baby outta one of these windows when we get inside."

"And Panama," I said meekly. I was still in pain from getting whacked upside the head and my only concern at that point was my daughter's safety.

"Who?"

"Panama. My mother's *man*."

"Where they at in the house?"

"I'm not sure."

Whack.

The dude slapped me upside the head with the gun again.

"I told you don't fucking lie to me!"

I looked and saw what looked like droplets of blood dripping onto my steps, and that freaked the shit outta me.

"My moms is upstairs, and Panama usually stays on the first floor."

"Aight. Open up this motherfucka," the guy ordered me before telling his boys that he wanted one of them to take upstairs, and the other one to check out the first floor.

My hand was shaking as I held my keys and moved them toward the lock. I was wondering if I should just take the L and get shot the fuck up right there on the steps and sacrifice my life for my mother's and my daughter's. But there was no time to think.

"Hurry up, bitch," the guy whispered into my ear with a growl in his voice.

I finally got the door open, and I turned on the lights for the foyer and the hallway. The guy with the gun walked behind me with his hand around my mouth and his gun in my back. The other two guys had their guns drawn, and they headed to the other parts of the house. The house was deathly silent.

Moments later I heard my mother's door being kicked open.

"Bitch, don't fucking move!" I heard the guy upstairs yell, and at the same time I heard my daughter break out into a terrifying cry.

"This ain't a dream, homey. Get the fuck on the ground," the other guy yelled loudly at a sleeping Panama.

"What the fuck?" Panama said, waking up to the barrel of a gun. He looked startled; he had clearly been sound asleep.

"Nigga, fuck you. Who the fuck are you, running up in my shit like this? Do you know who I am?" Panama said as the guy who had the gun on me walked me fully into the living room so that he could see what was going on.

Just as we were walking into the living room I saw the guy swing his gun and knock Panama right in his mouth. Blood flew from Panama's mouth like he had been hit by a blow from a heavyweight fighter.

"Nigga, I know who the fuck you *was*. You ain't shit now, motherfucka. Get yo' punk ass on the fucking floor right now before I blast yo punk old-school ass. You fucking snitch bitch."

Right then and there I knew that all of my fears about Panama had been confirmed. God damn. My mother shoulda believed me about Panama. She didn't, and look where it got our asses, I thought to myself.

Panama was butt-ass naked but he laid down on the floor like he was told, his balls exposed. He followed their orders.

"All right. Just don't hurt the baby," I heard my mother yell over the footsteps coming down the stairs.

"Get the fuck downstairs and hurry up," the guy yelled at my mother and my daughter, who was still crying.

"Get on the ground next to his ass. You, too," the guy who had held the gun on my mother ordered the two of us.

So Panama, my mother, my daughter, and I were all lying facedown on the hardwood living room floor, nervous as shit. I was just hoping that we all didn't get murdered execution-style.

"We gonna make this quick. Where the fuck is the stash at?" the guy who had originally rushed me outside asked.

Nobody said anything. The only thing that could be heard was my baby crying.

The guy who had hit Panama in the head cocked his gun to intimidate us into talking.

"The first room upstairs on your right, in the closet. Underneath a pile of clothes and shoes you'll see a cash box," I blurted out. I was referring to my private stash box, which held about $7,000 in cash. My hope was that they would take that money and bounce so that the $50,000 that my moms had stashed would be safe.

One of the guys immediately ran upstairs to my room and I heard him rumbling around and throwing shit all over the place. Two minutes or so later he came back.

"Yo, she trying to fuck us. Look at this shit."

"What?" I asked nervously, thinking that the money wasn't there or something.

"This is only like five grand. I know they holding more cash up in this bitch."

"That's all we got. I'm telling you," I pleaded.

"Get the fuck up," the ringleader yelled at me as he yanked me up by my hair.

I got to my feet and he nodded at the dude who had gone upstairs to retrieve the money, and then he looked in my direction.

"You wanna hit this shit?" he asked. "She trying to fuck us. But we running this shit, so let's fuck *her*."

Without hesitation the guy who had gone to retrieve the money from my closet came up behind me and reached both of his hands around my waist and started to yank at the button and zipper to my jeans. He still had the gun in his right hand and I instinctively tried to grab hold of it. I did grab it, and we started to tussle over it.

Click clack.

That's the sound I heard as the ringleader pointed his gun at my head. "Stop the bullshit and pull your fucking pants down!" he yelled.

I stopped dead and thought for a moment. I had

very few options, so I blew some air outta my lungs in frustration and then I said, "Yo, I can't believe y'all niggas is on that bitch-ass shit. Y'all gonna take my pussy, too?"

"Wait. Just hold up. Hold up. I got cash upstairs, just leave her alone," my mother screamed.

At that point my pants were already unzipped and unbuttoned so the guy I had been tussling with he grabbed my pants and literally ripped them off of me with one strong-ass pull. He left me standing there with ripped jeans and wearing only my red thong.

"Yo, leave her the fuck alone! We gonna get you your bread," Panama screamed from his spot on the floor.

"Nigga, shut the fuck up!" the ringleader said and kicked Panama in the mouth. "Where the cash at?" he demanded to know from my mother.

Meanwhile, the guy who had ripped my jeans began palming and feeling on my ass.

"Look, I said I'll tell you where the cash is at, but y'all gotta leave her the fuck alone!" my mother yelled.

The ringleader nodded for his man to back up off me.

After a pause my mother cursed into the air.

She lay on the floor barefoot, in a pair of white boy-short underwear and a T-shirt. She was clutching my daughter.

"Upstairs, the third door on your left. Look under the bed and you'll see a briefcase with money in it. That's all we got," my mother said through clenched teeth.

The third masked man in the room left us in the living room and bolted upstairs while the guy who had ripped my jeans stood next to me rubbing his crotch. "This that same fat ass that be up in the spot grinding up on niggas. Your shit looks a whole lot better up close and personal," the guy said to me while rubbing his dick.

"Hey, yo. Jack-Mother-Fucking-Pot," the guy who had gone upstairs yelled out as he came running back downstairs. "Come on, y'all let's get up outta here."

My mother looked like she was ready to kill but there was nothing she could do. On the other hand, Panama's bitch ass looked calm as a motherfucker, and it made me suspicious. But at that point I just wanted them niggas up outta my crib, and I was thankful that my daughter hadn't been hurt.

"Nah, chill for a minute," the guy next to me

said. The bandanna was still covering his face but I could picture his sinister smile and imagine him licking his lips like LL Cool J as he lusted over my fat ass.

"This bitch got my dick all hard and shit. Bend that ass over," he screamed at me.

"Nah, fuck that! Y'all got what y'all came for, now get the fuck up outta here," I said, resisting.

"Bend yo' ass over, bitch!" the guy screamed at me, forcefully placing his gun behind my ear and pushing my head down at the same time.

"You gonna have to kill me up in here before I let this go down," my mother shouted as she struggled to get up off the floor.

"Ma, just hold Nina!" I screamed in more fear of my daughter's safety than mines.

"Lay yo' ass down before I lay that ass out," the ringleader shouted at my mother while the guy who was harassing me ripped off my thong.

Thaa. Thaa.

When I heard the sound I turned and realized that the guy who was attacking me had chucked two globs of spit into my pussy, trying to lubricate it.

"Ahhh, motherfucker," I screamed when the dude rammed his dick into me doggy-style. My baby, who had been quiet, immediately started to scream and cry when she heard me scream.

I couldn't believe that Panama was just lying there, watching me get raped right in front of my mother and daughter.

"Y'all bitches talk all that shit and can't take no dick," the dude barked while he continued to pump his dick in and outta me. I grimaced in pain.

As I was getting raped and my baby was crying, Panama suddenly got up and bolted toward the living room window and literally dove right through the glass, butt-ass naked. Glass shattered from the first-floor window and splattered everywhere as Panama crashed to the ground outside. He had bolted and flown through the window so quickly that nobody really knew what was going on.

"Oh, shit. Come on. Come on. We gotta get that nigga and get the fuck up outta here."

The guy who was raping me pulled outta me and pulled his pants up and bounced outta the crib with his crew.

"Chyna, you all right?" my mother asked me.

"Yeah, yeah, I'm okay," I said as I immediately ran to pick up my daughter.

"Somebody is dying early this morning. I swear

to God!" my mother said as she ran upstairs to get her gun and her car keys.

"Chyna, stay here with Nina. Call Shanice, call Lorenzo, call everybody and tell them to come to the crib. Call P.J. and tell him to call me on the cell phone. I gotta go see where these niggas went," my mother shouted as she ran outta the house, half-dressed and wearing some black mesh slippers that she'd quickly put on her feet. "Don't nobody come up in my motherfucking crib and disrespect me like that. *Nobody,*" my mother raged.

I didn't want my moms to see me break down and look weak, but as soon as she left I ran and dialed my baby's father, Lorenzo, and told him what happened. I broke down and cried on the phone as the reality of what had just happened to me started to sink in.

"Baby, they raped me in front of Nina," I said as tears streamed down my face and I broke down to Lorenzo what had happened.

"Yo, Chyna, I swear on Nina's life I will kill that snitch motherfucker for putting you and *my daughter* through some shit like that," Lorenzo vowed. He told me he was gonna leave his house in Astoria, Queens, and head right over to Harlem.

I continued to speak to Lorenzo on his cell phone while he got up and retrieved his car keys.

"But baby, I don't know if it was Panama for sure," I said as I started to calm down just a bit.

"Chyna, fuck that. That nigga is a snitch and he set y'all up. He knew what time you would be leaving the club, and he knew how much dough y'all was holding. It was a fucking setup. Trust me," Lorenzo said.

Unfortunately I couldn't help but believe Lorenzo. Panama had really done us dirtier than I ever thought he would. I just hoped my mother would see through all the bullshit and realize that the nigga she swore by had had us set up and raped and robbed and damn near killed.

Test My Gangsta

About fifteen minutes after I hung up the phone with Lorenzo, my mother and Panama both came storming back into the house like gangbusters. It sounded like they knocked the front door off the hinges trying to get inside.

"Chyna. Chyna!" my mother screamed out to me.

My heart started beating because I didn't know what was up so I quickly reached to the top of my closet, where I had my gun inside a lockbox.

"Chyna, get me some towels. Hurry up," my mother shouted.

After I grabbed my gun I laid my daughter down in her playpen and left my room. I made sure that I locked my bedroom door so that Nina would be safe, and then I bolted downstairs to see what all the ruckus was about.

"Chyna, I said get me some towels! Shit," my mother screamed at me.

I looked and all I saw was blood everywhere, on the floor and streaming from Panama's body. Panama was bleeding real bad from his right leg and his right arm. My mother was applying as much pressure to his arm as she could to stop the bleeding, but she didn't look like she was doing much.

I ran to the linen closet and grabbed four towels and ran my ass back to the living room where Panama was lying on the ground, howling in pain.

"Here, Ma," I said as I handed my mother the towels. "What happened? Did he get shot?" I asked that because I had heard gunshots not long after my mom ran out of the house behind the dudes who jacked us.

"Nah, he ain't get shot. Chyna, take this towel and put pressure on his leg so it'll stop bleeding," my mother frantically said to me as she simultaneously took one of the towels and covered up Panama's genitals, which were still exposed.

"What the fuck happened?" I said as I began to calm down.

"He sliced his shit open when he jumped out the window," my mother explained.

"Panama, this shit don't look like it's gonna stop. You gotta get to the hospital and get stitched up," my moms warned.

Right after that my mother's right hand man, P.J., who also served as her muscle, came into the house, along with one of my mother's best friends, Shanice. Shanice was like an aunt to me; that's how close she and my mother were.

"Y'all aight?" P.J. asked. "What the fuck happened?"

"Help me stop this bleeding first and then I'll tell y'all what went down," my mother answered.

"Damn, that's a lot of blood. Roxy, you gotta have him elevate his arm and his leg, and that'll help the blood stop flowing," Shanice explained. My mother quickly followed her suggestion.

I had to run and get more towels because the ones I'd brought had already been saturated with blood.

"Ahh, this shit is stinging like hell," Panama screamed.

I returned with more towels, and when Panama's leg was lifted in the air I got a better look at the cut and immediately I knew that he was gonna need stitches, like my mother had said. I could see the white meat in his thigh, and all kinds of other shit that you usually only see when a doctor cuts you open.

"Shanice, call an ambulance," I said while applying pressure to the wound.

"No, let's take him! I don't want five-o coming up in here, asking a million questions," my mother said. Panama continued to writhe in pain.

Shanice looked through Panama's stuff, trying to find something for him to put on, and P.J. offered to drive us to the hospital in his truck.

As we were tending to Panama's wounds and preparing him for the hospital, Lorenzo, who lived right on the other side of the Triborough Bridge, came into the crib's foyer, calling out my name. It didn't take long for him to find me; he just followed the blood trail into the living room.

"What's up?" Lorenzo asked. He was with one of his boys and he had a look on his face like he was ready for some shit to go down. "Where's my daughter? She okay?"

"Yeah, yeah, she's upstairs in my room in the playpen. I locked the door," I explained to Lorenzo just in case he was planning on going up to Nina's room to check on her.

"You okay?" he asked me.

I nodded my head.

"What the fuck is wrong with this nigga?" Lorenzo asked with a screw face.

"Lo! You know who this is?" my mother asked Lorenzo as she looked up at him from where she knelt, continuing to put pressure on Panama's wounds.

"I know who the fuck he is. He's the snitch-ass nigga that set y'all up," Lorenzo screamed. "You got niggas running up in here with gats and shit while my daughter is in her bed sleeping? What the fuck is you on?" Lorenzo asked Panama.

Panama immediately looked like he'd slipped into fight mode and despite his wounds he struggled to get to his feet, adjusting the towel around his waist.

"Panama, lay back down," my mother screamed at him.

P.J. walked back in the house and informed everybody that he had pulled his truck to the front of the house and was ready to go to the hospital.

"Nigga, do I know you? What the fuck you talking about, homey?" Panama said to Lorenzo, who approached Panama and stared him down. The towel that Panama had wrapped around his waist to hide his dick was also getting soaked with blood.

"Chyna, talk to Lorenzo. Panama, come on—let's go to the emergency room," my mother ordered.

At that moment Lorenzo's homeboy pulled out his gun and aimed it at Panama. "Test my gangsta if you want to, homey," he said to Panama.

"Yo, put that shit away!" my mother barked at the dude.

"Chill, I got this," Lorenzo said. "Roxy, I been silent on this shit for a while, but word is bond you fucking wit' a snitch-ass nigga right there. And I'm telling you, he set yo' ass up."

"Dog, I done killed many motherfuckers who showed me more respect than you showing me right now," Panama said as he approached Lorenzo.

"Lo, just chill the fuck out. Shanice, walk him to the truck with P.J., and I'ma come right over there to the hospital in a minute," my mother said.

Panama finally heeded his situation and made his way outta the house and into the truck so that he wouldn't bleed to death.

As soon as Panama was outta earshot Lorenzo spoke up. "Roxy, I ain't trying to disrespect your crib, but you dealing with a fraud-ass dude right there."

"Lo," my mother said as she buried her face in the palms of her hands. She paused for a moment before removing her hands from her face. Then she let out a yell of frustration. "My living room window is broke, there's fucking blood all throughout my shit, them niggas got me for fifty fucking thousand that I gotta get back, they raped my daughter—I ain't trying to entertain no beef and no bullshit right now!" she yelled.

"Ma, it ain't bullshit. Just hear him out."

"Chyna, not now. Aight?" my mother screamed.

"Chyna, let me just get Nina and take her to my crib. Holla at me later today," Lorenzo said to me while walking away and slowly shaking his head.

I gave Lorenzo the key to my bedroom so that he could unlock the door, and I followed my mother into the kitchen, where she cracked open a Heineken. I was getting tired of my mother's denial.

"Ma, how the dude just gonna lay there while them niggas was running all through our shit and raping me?" I asked, my voice raised.

My mother didn't look at me, and she didn't respond for a moment. She just stood there and drank her beer.

I exhaled with frustration before speaking again. "Ain't nobody know about that dough we was holding except for me, you, Panama, and the niggas that gave it to you. And the niggas that gave it to you don't know where the fuck we live at. Them cats knew we had more money—they kept pressing us after I had told them where my stash was at. But that wasn't enough for them. Ma, how can't you see it?" I screamed.

The next thing I knew my mother threw her Heineken bottle across the room as hard as she could and it smashed into the wall and shattered, sending beer and green shards of glass everywhere.

"Chyna, the niggas had guns to his fucking head. What the fuck was he supposed to do?" my mother asked.

"Take a fucking bullet. That's what he was supposed to do. The nigga is supposed to be so gangsta, but he was laying there looking like a straight bitch! How he gonna lay there while a nigga is poking my pussy right in front of my daughter?" I said in a sarcastic and angry tone. The reality of what had happened to me came flooding back to the front of my mind, making me angrier by the second. I suddenly realized that I had no idea how I had even brought myself to render any first aid to Panama's wounds.

"So him diving out the window, that shit was fake?" my mother asked.

I didn't respond.

"Chyna, he cut his leg going through that window butt-ass naked, and you know why he went through the window? He was going for his gun that was inside his truck. He made it to his truck and had to break the truck window with his goddamn elbow so he could get to the gun, and he gashed his arm in the process. Was that shit fake, too, Chyna?"

I still said nothing. I just looked at my mom.

"Chyna, I saw Panama bussing his gun at the niggas that ran up in here. They was driving off in an all-black Altima. And trust me, he was gunning for them niggas for real. He wasn't just firing shots into the air, purposely trying to miss. And when I got in my car he got in the shit bleeding like a motherfucker, and I know what he said to me. I know what he was saying while we was trying to hunt those niggas down. It was real talk, Chyna. I already told you to drop that whole snitching shit that Lorenzo is filling your head up wit'. And if I hear that shit again from you or from Lorenzo, y'all gonna have a problem with me. You understand that shit?"

I didn't respond. I just walked off more frustrated than ever and made my way upstairs to where Lorenzo and his man and the baby were.

As I walked off I heard my mother in the background talking under her breath, but she was purposely talking loud enough so that I could hear what she was saying: "Instead of her ass worrying about how gangsta somebody is, her ass needs to be worrying about helping her mother figure out how to get up this fucking money for this run I gotta make."

"Whateva," I said under my breath as I walked up the stairs. I was seconds from just walking out on my mother and going with Lorenzo and Nina to Queens and saying to hell with the whole Harlem Heat shit.

A big part of me felt like if my mother *wanted* to be in denial about Panama, and if she *wanted* to have her nose up his ass, then I was gonna let her do her thing and I would do mine on my own. I made good money dancing, and I didn't need no added drama from a snitch that my mother couldn't see through.

But at the end of the day, regardless of how I felt at the moment, after all the hurt and beef and bitching, my mother was still my flesh and blood, and she had always been down for me and taught me all that I knew—which is what made me the woman I was. So I knew that I couldn't flat leave her ass to sort shit out on her own. Nah, I couldn't just run to Queens and hide like a bitch, even though that was what a part of me felt like doing.

My mother and I had money to get, $50,000 that wasn't even our fucking money. We had to come up with a plan to get it back, and get it back quick. And if not, there was definitely gonna be some drama when the Bloods would start calling for their guns.

It was on.

My mother and I would have to come up with a plan together as a team, and then work that plan like a team. And I would try my best to block out my personal feelings about Panama and his suspect ass.

8

Let's Get
This Money

Late that afternoon, Panama, who had received thirtysomething stitches in his leg and another ten stitches in his arm, returned home from the emergency room and told my moms that he was bouncing and that he would be crashing with his man who was from Brownsville, Brooklyn.

Apparently Panama had a real issue with what went down between Lorenzo, Lorenzo's homeboy, and himself, and he wanted to escalate shit and bring it to Lorenzo and his people for disrespecting him.

So while my mother and I were brainstorming and trying to figure out how to get the money up, Panama, who had just gotten back from the hospital, walked through the front door and—in my opinion—*conveniently* used the beef with Lorenzo to put a wedge between him and my mother. Immediately he started raising hell with my moms. He was screaming and cursing at her, asking her how come she hadn't come to the hospital like she said she was gonna do.

"Panama, these niggas just jacked us for fifty thousand dollars and I'm stressed the fuck out sitting here trying to figure out how I'ma get this money back. That's why I didn't come," my mother shouted back at Panama in response to his anger toward her.

"You let them bitch-ass niggas play me out and put a gun to my head and then you stay here and chill wit' them and not come to the emergency room to see what was up with me?"

"Oh my God. Panama, why the fuck you even gotta go there? Do you see them still here? Lorenzo ain't here, and neither is his boy," my mother answered.

"Where the fuck them niggas live at, Roxy?" Panama demanded to know.

"Panama, let it go. That's my granddaughter's father. It's over. Forget about it."

"It ain't fucking over! Roxy, you know how I get down. Can't no nigga put a gun to my head and be walking around still breathing like shit is all good. Fuck that. Them niggas gotta bleed and feel some

pain."

"We need to be figuring out who the hell were them cats that ran up in the crib and got us for this money—."

"We gonna find that out!" Panama said, cutting her off. "But the first thing I wanna deal with is how I was fucking disrespected."

My mother blew some air outta her lungs and went to retrieve a cigarette. But she didn't say nothing.

"Roxy, word is bond. If you don't tell me where these niggas rest at, then I know you switching up sides on a nigga. Just let me know right the fuck now."

"Ugh. Panama, why the hell you even going there? You know me. Pete, you fucking know me, and you know how I do. You just gotta understand that if Lorenzo is involved in some shit then automatically my granddaughter is involved in the same shit."

Panama didn't say nothing else to my moms; he just started knocking shit around and moving shit like he was looking for something. What he was really doing was gathering his shit so that he could leave.

"Roxy, I ain't fucking wit' yo' ass. Fuck this shit," Panama said as he finished scooping up clothes and shoes and put them inside a huge black garbage bag and made his way to the front door. The clothes and shoes were the same clothes and shoes my mother had purchased for him, depleting her stash.

"Panama, just chill. Where you going?"

Panama didn't reply. He just continued making his way to the front door so that he could leave. My mother ran behind him and pushed the door closed to prevent him from leaving.

"Babe, relax. Just chill. Why the fuck you leaving?" my mother asked with a nervous smile plastered across her face.

Panama looked at her with a screw face and said, "Roxy, on the real, if I don't leave now we gonna have an issue. Me and you. You knaimean?"

"What?" My mother shook her head before speaking again. "Okay, wait, wait, wait. First of all, I don't know what you mean. And where the hell are you going?"

At that point Panama moved my mother outta the way and told her that he was going to his man's crib in Brownsville.

"I ain't fucking wit' you, Roxy. You on that bullshit," he said as he strolled off and hopped in the Denali that my mother had paid for.

My mother just stood there at the top of the stoop looking at him until he drove off. When Panama's truck was no longer in sight she came back in the crib.

"Fuck his ass, Ma!" I shouted to my mother as she closed the front door. I knew exactly what Panama was doing, and my mother had to know, too. He was acting like the lame-ass dudes who break up with their chicks a week before Valentine's day so that they'll have a built-in excuse for not buying them shit. Only Panama was bouncing from my mom's crib so that he could put that $50,000 in the street to work for him while being outta my mother's sight.

My mother came back into the living room and bowed her head and closed her eyes while pinching the bridge of her nose with the index finger and thumb of her right hand. She was clearly stressed the fuck out.

"Nah, Chyna, I wanted that nigga to help us get this money back. Shit. I don't know what we gonna do, but we gotta get this gwop," my mother said in a surrendered and defeated tone.

I walked up to her and hugged her and said, "So let's do what we gotta do, and *let's get this money.*"

9

Bonnie & Clyde
aka
Roxy & Chyna

By that Wednesday, two days after we'd been robbed, I had hustled up about two grand dancing in the club. It was enough money to buy diapers and food and replace the broken window in the living room and buy disinfectants to clean up all the blood that Panama had spilled throughout our house and inside my mother's car, but that's about as far as that two grand took us.

Not including the money that had been stolen from me personally, my mother and I were still fifty grand in the hole, and we needed to get that fifty grand by Friday so that we could head to Georgia and purchase the guns that we had to deliver to the Bloods by Saturday.

There weren't too many people me or my mother could turn to who would just cough up fifty grand overnight and not want a whole lot of unnecessary shit in return for it. Because of my reputation and my mother's reputation we didn't want to start hitting up all our friends for one thousand dollars here and one thousand dollars there, because it would've made us look weak, and the perception would have been that we were dead broke.

Besides, as far as my mother was concerned, borrowing the money didn't make much sense because all it would have meant was that once we gathered up the fifty grand to buy the guns and completed the transaction there would be no profit for us. The fifty grand in profit that we would've stood to make would have gone right back out of our hands to repay the people we'd borrowed it from.

"Chyna, we gotta get this money Bonnie and Clyde style," my mother said to me while I fed Nina her formula. "But we gonna do it smart. We gonna hit three or four banks out on Long Island and get like fifteen thousand from each bank, and we'll be good. This way we ain't gotta pay back shit to nobody and we'll be making money off this deal," my mother explained.

The first thing that came to my mind was that my mother was buggin' if she thought that we could rob three banks and not get caught. One, maybe—but three? It just sounded too unrealistic and with my daughter being as young as she was I had to think about the consequences if we were to get caught. The risks didn't outweigh the rewards.

"Three banks?" I asked as I patted Nina on her back, trying to burp her.

My mother nodded her head and then got up and went to her bedroom. When she returned she had on a pair of stylish gloves and she was holding three white index cards.

"You see this?" she asked while holding up the cards.

"Yeah."

"This is our fifty thousand dollars right here," my mom said as she searched for a pen.

"This is how we gonna do this. Me, you, and Nina are gonna head out to Long Island and hit a Arco National Bank branch, a North Shore Savings Bank branch, and a Nassau County Credit Union branch. I want us to go to Long Island because out there the bank tellers don't be behind those bulletproof partitions and all that."

I listened and looked at my mother intently as I continued to burp Nina.

"And since they ain't got those partitions and all that, all I gotta do is pass the teller a note saying I got a gun in my bag and for them to give up the dough. They'll take my ass serious and give up the cash without any problems, just like they're trained to do."

"But what about cameras and all that?"

"I'll have on shades and I'll probably wear a different hat and a different top for each bank that we hit. I don't know, but fuck the cameras, though—it won't matter," my mother insisted.

I blew some air out of my lungs and shook my head as I laid Nina down on the couch so that she could sleep.

"Ma, I don't know."

"Chyna, you don't know what? Don't bitch up on my ass now. It ain't like we got a whole bunch of options," my mother said as I sat and thought about everything she was saying.

"Chyna, I'll go inside the banks. All you gotta do is just sit outside in the car with Nina and wait for my ass to come out. You'll be driving, and when I leave with the money I'll get in the passenger seat and we'll pull off and it'll be all good."

I didn't respond and my mother looked at me but didn't say anything else. She simply sat down and started writing on the three index cards.

She paused in her writing and looked at me and explained that she knew for a fact that all bank tellers usually hold like fifteen grand, and that they are trained to just give up the money without hesitation.

"Chyna, it won't be nothing. If we was trying to come off with like five hundred thousand or some big figure like that then I would say that we couldn't easily pull that off. But this? It won't be nothing."

"So you already thought this whole thing through?" I asked my moms.

"You see these damn gloves on my hands, right?"

I nodded my head.

"I ain't trying to leave no fingerprints or slip up in no way, baby. All last night I tossed and turned in my sleep just thinking about if and how we could pull this off."

I sighed and looked over at my daughter, who looked so peaceful as she slept. And I knew that if we hit those banks and didn't do it right that my daughter's peaceful sleep—and her life—would be rudely interrupted while I rotted in jail.

"What about the silent alarms and dye packs and all of that?" I asked my mother.

"Each bank that we hit they're gonna activate their alarms—that's without question. But I'll be in and outta there so quick that it won't matter. And the dye packs—we can't worry about that, 'cause not all tellers even have that shit," my mother reasoned.

I didn't respond or comment. I just walked to the kitchen to get something to eat since it was breakfast time and I hadn't eaten anything since coming home from the strip club a few hours earlier.

After I'd been in the kitchen alone for about ten minutes my mother walked up to me and held out one of the index cards for me to read, but she wouldn't let me touch it.

It read: *This is not a joke! So don't let my nice clothes, my smile, or my pretty face fool you. Don't panic and don't look around. Take this plastic bag and put all of the money that you have inside of it. I got a gun pointed right at you but if you cooperate I won't have to use it.*

"Wow. Ma, this is crazy," I said after reading the note and putting a spoonful of cold cereal in my mouth.

"What? You think it won't work?"

"Nah, it ain't that. I know it'll work. I just can't believe you're really dead-ass about it."

"Chyna, I ain't bullshitting," my mother replied. "Matter of fact, hurry up and finish eating and get dressed and then get Nina ready. We gotta bounce and do this shit *today!* If we leave by like eleven this morning we can be out there by twelve noon, and that'll give us enough time to hit all three banks. Plus, I don't want you changing your mind on me."

I looked up at my mother and she walked off, back toward the living room, saying that she was gonna go on the internet and get the addresses of the banks and that we would use the navigational system in the car to get there.

"Chyna, hurry up!" she shouted.

I closed my eyes and sighed and paused for a moment, realizing that my mother was really 'bout it 'bout it. I shook my head but decided to just trust that my mother wouldn't get us into no shit that we wouldn't be able to get out of. I left my cereal right there on the table, half-eaten, and I got up. Wearing an oversized T-shirt that hung down around my thighs, I made my way upstairs to the shower so that I could get dressed and ready to handle business with my mother.

It took me about forty-five minutes to get myself and my daughter ready. And in that same time my mother had also gotten ready. I was wearing Cartier Aviator gold-rimmed shades, high-heel black over-the-knee Bottega Veneta boots, along with a Stella McCartney cashmere shawl cardigan and a Stella McCartney liquid jersey dress. I carried a matching Bottega Veneta oversized leather python bag.

My mother was wearing a dark blue three-piece John Galliano suit—a checked blazer and classic pinstriped pants, and a fitted wool shirt—along with oversized Chanel shades, a floppy wide-brim suede hat, and a Badgley Mischka leather tote bag with matching heels.

The two of us looked like high-powered fashion executives, and there was no way in the world that if anyone were to see us in the street they would suspect that we were capable of robbing a bank. And the thing was, that was just how me and my moms rolled on a regular, so it was like second nature for us to rock the high-end shit that we were rocking.

"Ma, you should take my bag and let me take yours since mines is bigger," I said to my mother as I applied my lip gloss.

My mother agreed, and we switched bags. When I was done applying my lip gloss I grabbed hold of Nina, who was also dressed in a nice little outfit, and I placed a bib around her and prepared to walk out to the car with her and put her in the car seat.

"I'll be out there in five minutes," my mother said to me as she began applying makeup to her face.

It was bright and sunny outside, though somewhat brisk; for the most part it was a perfect day, weather-wise.

"Hey, you little princess. You're such a cutie pie," I said to my daughter playfully as I pinched her cheeks and made her laugh.

I tried my hardest to block out what my mother and I were on our way to do because I knew that if I thought about it I would not go through with it.

"I love you, too, pookie-poo. You love mommy? Huh? You do? Yeah?"

I reached my mother's car and deactivated the alarm, and then I strapped my daughter into her seat. I went around to the driver's side and got in and turned on the ignition and sat and listened to music on the radio.

"We got this, Nina. Mommy and grandma got this, okay, sweetie-pie?" I turned and said to my daughter. She looked at me all wide-eyed and started to laugh and smile.

"We gonna get this money and come back home so I can give you a bath and then mommy is going to sleep," I explained to Nina as I talked to her in an effort to calm my nerves.

Before long my mother came outside and got in the front passenger's side of the car.

"Yo, I can't believe we even gotta do this shit. I'ma find out who them niggas were that ran up in our crib the other night. You best believe that shit," my mother said to me before instructing me to head toward the Triborough Bridge so that we could get on the Grand Central Parkway. She then put the visor down so that she could look at herself in the mirror while she put her lipstick on.

"I put some Bacardi and Coke in this bottle right here if you want some."

I shook my head no and just kept driving. My mother explained how we were gonna go about hitting each spot. She also told me that there were a screwdriver and some other tools in the trunk, and that the first thing that we would have to do when we got to Long Island was find a car and take the license plates off of that car and switch them to our

HARLEM HEAT

car just in case anybody were to get a look at the car we were in.

Although it was still relatively early in the day, my mother soon began throwing back the Bacardi and Coke like she was guzzling a bottle of Poland Spring water.

"I can't go up in these banks sober," my mother explained to me.

I looked over at her but didn't say anything. Her words didn't surprise me because I knew that she was human, and no matter how much ice she had flowing through her veins there was just no way that she couldn't have been shook, even if she was just a little bit shook about what we were about to do.

After about forty minutes of driving, the navigation system directed us to a mini shopping plaza that was located in Great Neck, Long Island—the site of our Arco National Bank branch. But my mother and I didn't immediately drive into the shopping plaza; instead we circled the area until we located a Honda Accord that was parked in an isolated area. My mother jumped out and quickly swiped the license plates of the Honda and put them on the BMW we were driving. Then she hid the BMW plates underneath the spare tire in our trunk. When we were done with that we headed back to the shopping plaza where the bank was located.

"Aight, that's the bank right over there," my mother told me as she pointed to the bank.

I forget exactly what time it was, and the fact is, I wasn't exactly thinking about a clock. My mind was preoccupied with being on the lookout for cops and anyone who might be looking at our car in a suspicious manner.

Located within the shopping plaza along with the bank were a supermarket, a Chinese restaurant, a health club, and other little convenience shops. The shopping plaza's parking lot was just about full to capacity, and the only available parking spaces were like a fifty-yard walk from the bank.

"We can't park all the way over here," my mother said to me, her voice low, as she scanned the parking lot for other spots.

"Since I'm staying in the car I'll just park in one of those handicapped spots."

"Oh, okay, good. Definitely that's it," my mother said to me as she looked around inside the car and inside her bag and double- and triple-checked everything.

"You think these gloves are too much?" she asked me.

"Nah, it flows with the outfit, and plus you don't have a choice. They won't be paying attention to that, anyway."

After I made it into the handicapped spot my mother paused. Then she sighed.

"Okay, this is the deal. I got your number on speed dial. If I call you for any reason, even if we don't speak on the phone, it means that something went wrong and I want you to get the fuck up outta dodge with Nina. Aight?"

I nodded my head and without hesitation my mother exited the car and made her way toward the bank. I blew some air outta my lungs and then I looked in the backseat at Nina. She looked so peaceful as she slept. That girl could sleep through a plane crash, I thought and chuckled to myself.

At that point my cell phone started ringing. My heart immediately dropped. I looked at the caller ID but—thank God—it wasn't my mom, so I let it go to voicemail. My heart was beating fast as hell and I was hoping that everything was going smooth for my mother inside the bank. But my nerves couldn't take it and I grabbed the Bacardi and Coke that my mom had been drinking and started guzzling it down in the hope of calming my nerves. I couldn't relax for shit and kept switching the radio from station to station.

Then from out of nowhere, I saw my mother emerge from the bank, holding my leather python bag and looking sexy and sophisticated as hell. She was quickly approaching the car. With her hat and shades on I couldn't read the expression on her face but I sensed that everything was okay.

My mother got in the car and sat down and immediately told me to drive off.

"Go, Chyna, let's get the fuck up outta here!"

Without hesitation and without asking any questions I put the car in reverse and started to back up, but I instantly jammed on the brakes because there was a car directly behind me that had me sort of boxed in from a perpendicular angle.

"Oh, shit! You believe this motherfucker?" I screamed out and instantly started blowing on the horn for the car to move. "Goddamn, it's some fucking old people!" I said to my mother.

"Chyna, I got this money—we gotta go. Pull off! Just go!"

"Ma, you want me to ram their car?" I asked.

"Ah, shit. Chyna, two people just came from outta the bank. Just drive!" my mother hollered.

I was about to roll down my window and scream for the old couple to get out of my way, but there was no time for that—the two men who had emerged from the bank were looking around, and they pointed in the direction of our car.

I threw the car in drive and hit the accelerator and took the car right up on the curb and almost rammed right into the storefront window of the Chinese res-taurant. I then threw the car in reverse, backed up a few feet, and put the car back in drive. I literally drove down the length of the sidewalk of the shop-ping plaza until I could maneuver the car back into the main traffic lanes of the parking lot.

The car was bouncing and banging into concrete and the ride was bumpy. People were running and diving for cover so that they wouldn't get hit by our out-of-control car.

"Ma, which way?" I asked nervously. I had just realized that we'd never taken the time to plan our escape route.

"Go straight and make that left at the light. Run the light. Just run it!" my mother screamed. All the bumpiness and the commotion woke my daughter, and she started to cry. She wasn't wailing; her cry sounded more like she was annoyed.

I hit the gas and the car's tires screeched and I blew the light and made my left turn and came within inches of ramming like three cars.

"Just go straight until you see the Long Island Expressway," my mother said to me as she took off her shades and the hat and threw her head back and ran both of her hands down her face, as if she was in anguish. "Chyna, we got them motherfuckers!" my mother screamed.

I was too nervous to respond to her, and too worried about making it to the expressway before coming across a damn cop.

"It gotta be at least fifteen G's in this bag," my mother said to me as she held open the bag for me to see all the cash.

"Yeah, no question," I said quickly as I entered the entrance ramp of the expressway and headed east, farther out onto Long Island.

"Go three exits and then pull off and find a residential block and just park," my mother said to me, continually looking in the rearview and side-view mirrors to see if anyone was following us.

I did as my mother said, and we soon found ourselves parked in front of an immaculate suburban home with a manicured lawn and the whole nine.

The neighborhood was apparently so exclusive that no one parked their cars on the curb. Instead, all the cars were parked in huge driveways, which meant that we could have easily stood out.

"You got something for Nina to eat? Give her a pacifier or something," my mother said to me, as Nina was still crying in the backseat.

I reached and gave Nina her bottle. My mother told me to pop the trunk, and she went to the trunk to hide the money. She returned quickly since we did stick out in the pristine area.

"Aight, we can't stay here. Let's bounce," my mother said. I pulled off and we made our way back to the Long Island Expressway and headed toward our second bank.

My mother finally cracked a smile. "Chyna, that shit was so fucking easy I couldn't believe it. Yo, you shoulda saw the look on that white chick's face when I handed her the note. I smiled at her because I was nervous but I know she must've thought that I was some crazy-ass black bitch ready to blow her head off."

"So she just gave up the dough with no resistance?" I asked.

My mother looked at me and smiled even wider as she asked me for a pound. "No resistance at all," she said, clasping my hand.

After that we spoke about how we had screwed up by not having mapped out a getaway route, and by letting that car box us in. But it was all good because by the time we hit our second and third banks we had learned from our mistakes from the first bank, and we had everything down to a science by that point.

In fact, the robberies of the second and third banks went so smoothly that as we maneuvered our way onto the Southern State Parkway so that we could head back to Harlem, we joked that we probably had been in the wrong hustle all along and that we seriously needed to think about doing this bank-robbing hustle on a full-time basis, or at least as a supplement to our current money.

"Chyna, we gotta have at least forty grand in that trunk right now, if not more," my mother said to me. "Thank God we ain't gotta worry about getting these niggas they shit. Yo, this had me so stressed the fuck out."

I could tell that she was happy and relieved. But then she threw me off with what she did next. She started dialing on her cell phone. "Panama, what's up, baby? This is Roxy. Hit me back. Hurry up. I got that money up and I want you to come wit' me and Chyna outta state to make this run. Get off that bitch-ass shit and call me back," my mother said, apparently leaving a message for Panama.

I shook my head and couldn't believe that my mother had actually called that nigga.

"He better hurry up and call me back."

I wanted to talk about anything other than Panama, so I asked my mom where was I taking the Southern State Parkway to.

"It's gonna split into the Belt Parkway and the Cross Island Parkway. Take the Cross Island Parkway north," my mother replied.

At that point we had just passed exit 17 on the Southern State Parkway. I didn't want to overreact and panic, but I was sure that like five cars back and two lanes over was the same state trooper's patrol car that I had seen like three exits prior, so I had to say something to my mother.

"Ma, I think we being followed by the jakes."

"What?"

"I don't know for sure, but there's a state trooper like five or six cars back and I been seeing his car for like the past three exits now. I think he following us, but he's trying to act like he ain't."

My mother slowly turned and looked until she was able to spot the state trooper.

"Motherfucker. Chyna, I forgot to switch the damn plates back. Shit!" my mother said as she banged the palms of her hands on the dashboard.

At that moment her cell phone began vibrating.

"Damn, this is Panama," my mother said to me before answering the phone. "Hello, Panama, what's good?" my mother said. I could hear the nervous energy in her voice. She paused for a moment from speaking on the phone, and then she took another look to see where the state trooper was. "Yeah, I got that money up that them dudes juxed me for the other night. . ."

I couldn't believe that my mother was so dumb and that she was spilling the beans to Panama that quick. But I couldn't worry about that at the moment. I had more pressing concerns. I tapped my mother on the leg and whispered to her that the cop had switched lanes. I motioned for her to look in the rearview mirror.

"Panama, I gotta bounce. Something just came up, but yo, I'll hit you back," my mother said as she abruptly hung up her cell phone.

"Goddamn! This nigga is trying to get in our ass. Shit," my mother barked. "Just drive and try

not to be nervous," my mother said to me in a panicked tone.

"Nah, I'm good, I ain't nervous," I lied, as I
quickly glanced over my shoulder at my daughter. I
shook my head and my heart felt like it had just sunk
to my feet. I knew for sure that I was about to go to
jail and that it would probably be a long time before
I would see my daughter again. In my heart I knew
that I had fucked up at the first bank and brought too
much attention to us by driving all crazy and on the
sidewalk and shit.

The state trooper accelerated, and then he was in
the same lane as we were in. At that point there was
just one car separating his patrol car from us. I turned
the volume down on the music so that I could con-
centrate better on the reality of what was going on.
Then, before I knew it, the one car that separated our
BMW from the state trooper's car decided to switch
lanes, leaving the state trooper directly behind me.
And at that point the state trooper literally had his
patrol car inches from my bumper and he was purposely trying to intimidate me.

I can't front. I was nervous as hell . . .

Cold-blooded
Divas

By the time my mother and I made it back to Harlem it was a little past five in the evening. We were both so stressed out that we had to stop and get some weed to help calm our nerves.

On the ride home we had come up with a game plan on how we were gonna deal with the bank robberies and the cop killing if we were ever questioned by the police. Basically, we were gonna deny everything. There was no way that we were gonna admit to shit. We knew that there was no way that anyone could have any kind of fingerprint evidence on us since my mom had been wearing gloves throughout the whole ordeal.

And even if people could ID our BMW, the car

couldn't positively be linked back to us because we had switched the plates. As far as someone getting a glimpse of what we looked like, we weren't too worried about that because we'd both had on shades, and my mom's hat did a good job of disguising who she was. As far as an alibi, we agreed that we would swear to no end that we had been home all day long, sleeping and taking care of my baby. That would be our story and we would stick to it no matter what.

"We gotta shred the rest of those index cards and throw 'em in the garbage," my mother said to me as soon as we walked in the front door.

Nina was way overdue for a diaper change, so I immediately took care of her.

"Hurry up and take off those clothes and them boots and them shades and all of that and give 'em to me. I'ma take all this shit and the shredded index cards over to Shanice's crib and burn this shit and stash most of the money over there. And I'll tell her to take the BMW and park it in that parking garage on the west side, near midtown, and let it lay up in there for a few weeks, knaimean?" my mother explained to me.

I didn't think twice about my mother's choice of Shanice's crib to get rid of anything incriminating.

Shanice was as real as they came, and if there was one thing she wasn't it was a snitch. She had been through just about everything with my mother and I and she often went back and forth outta town, helping us run guns.

Before I could get my daughter's diaper fully off of her, my cell phone started ringing. At almost the exact same time my mother's cell phone also started ringing.

"Don't answer the phone, and don't talk to nobody just yet," my mother warned me. "I don't care if it's Panama, Lorenzo, or whoever. Just let the shit go to voicemail."

I nodded my head in agreement and attempted to continue changing Nina's diaper. But as soon as my cell phone stopped ringing, it started again. And almost simultaneously our home phone started ringing.

"What the fuck?" my mother screamed, as her cell phone had started ringing, too.

Apparently everybody was trying to get in touch with us all of a sudden, and I knew that it couldn't be a coincidence.

"Ma, both of the numbers on my caller ID were different numbers. Your cell is ringing off the hook, the home phone is ringing all of a sudden, and don't nobody call us on our home number. Something is up," I said. My heart rate picked up and I quickly finished changing Nina's diaper.

Ten minutes went by, and there were no other phone calls. My mother had rounded up all the expensive-ass gear that we had worn earlier, and I couldn't believe that she was actually going to go burn them, my fly-ass boots and all. It almost brought tears to my eyes to see such nice high-end gear going to waste. But before she could leave the house my cell phone started to ring yet again.

"Ma, it's Lo, I'm answering it," I said, and I answered before my mother had a chance to respond.

"Hello," I said into the phone.

"Chyna, what the fuck is going on? I had like three niggas just call me, talking about the police got a videotape on the news of these chicks shooting that cop out on Long Island today and everybody is saying it looks just like you and Roxy."

At that point my body felt like it had suddenly gone limp and like I was gonna fall out or some shit but I managed to play things off. I smiled in the hope that my smile would somehow break through the phone.

"Get the fuck outta here!" I said to Lorenzo while my mother was motioning for me to hang up the phone.

"Me and my moms been up in this damn house all day long with Nina, so that definitely wasn't us."

Lorenzo was quiet for a minute.

"So where's Nina?"

"She laying right here smiling up a storm. I just finished changing her." I paused and then I continued, "Yo, that's too funny, though, what you just asked me. Nigga, you know I woulda told you some shit like that."

I didn't want to but I know that I was sounding kind of nervous.

"Gimme this damn phone," my mother mumbled in a tone that was audible only to me while snatching my cell phone out of my hand and pressing the end button.

"I told you don't pick up the fucking phone, and you on there running your fucking mouth."

"Ma, that was Lo asking me about a fucking videotape that the cops is showing on the news of us shooting the cop," I hollered back.

My mother looked at me and closed her eyes and threw her head back. She thought to herself in silence for a few minutes, and then she turned on the television. The five o'clock news was just ending, and the six o'clock news was just starting.

The first words that came out of the news anchorwoman's mouth were "Cold-blooded divas."

The anchorwoman then went on in great detail, explaining how a massive manhunt was on for two nicely dressed women who were wanted in connection with the cold-blooded murder of a state trooper earlier in the day in Elmont, Long Island. She then mentioned that the same women were also wanted in connection with a string of bank robberies that had taken place on Long Island only hours before the state trooper had been killed.

As they showed the surveillance video from the bank's cameras and from the state trooper's dashboard camera, it was pretty clear that the same woman—*my mother*—who had been robbing the banks was also the woman who had pulled the trigger and shot the cop. My face was also visible despite the shades that I had on.

Before the news was done with the story, our cell phones began ringing again like crazy.

"Chyna, *do not* answer the phone!" my mother shouted like a dog that had gone mad. "Go get the keys to your truck and grab some diapers and bottles for Nina. Just follow me. We gotta bounce outta town. Shit is way too hot," my mother said to me as she turned the television off.

I didn't say anything, and I didn't ask any questions. I just listened to my mother's instructions word for word. And within five minutes my daughter and I had piled into my Mercedes truck and my mother had jumped into her BMW. I followed behind my mother as she took the BMW to a midtown parking garage that wasn't too far from the Lincoln Tunnel. After she'd parked the BMW she came and got in my truck with a bag full of money and we entered the Lincoln Tunnel and headed south on the New Jersey Turnpike. We were desperately trying to make our way outta town.

In a matter of hours our faces had become infamous, and we had instantly become New York's most wanted.

We were on the run.

And for my daughter's sake I was hoping that we wouldn't get bagged. 'Cause if we did, we would definitely be going up for life.

No Honor
Among Thieves

*A*fter stopping only for gas and once at a motel in North Carolina to rest, my mother, Nina, and I made our way to the one-bedroom apartment we'd always kept in my name down in Atlanta to maintain our residency requirements for the state of Georgia.

The three of us were officially on the run from the law. But what was wild was that what we had done in New York was quickly turning into a national story. When we had stopped at the motel to rest, we were in our room and I turned on CNN and saw our story on a world news channel. And it was then that the magnitude of what we had done really hit home. In fact, the CNN report went a step further than all the other news reports by specifically mentioning my mother's name. CNN stated that "the cops had been previously investigating the Harlem Heat gunrunning ring, which Roxy Reynolds also allegedly heads."

With all the notoriety, my mother thought that it would be best if for like two or three weeks we didn't contact anybody we knew. She even wanted us to find a brand-new apartment in Atlanta so that we would virtually disappear off the face of the earth. So during our second day in Atlanta, that was exactly what we did. For the whole ride to Atlanta we had kept our cell phones turned off, and we had no intention of using them. Instead, we had stopped and bought four prepaid cell phones.

We had all the money that we had stolen from the banks with us. And in all, we counted a little over $39,000 dollars that we had at our disposal. So from that we took five grand and bought a used Volkswagen Jetta. For obvious reasons it didn't make much sense to be driving around in a flashy car with New York plates; that would do nothing but attract unwanted attention to ourselves.

So for the next two and a half to three weeks we really didn't have much of a life. Other than going to the supermarket to get food or to the mall to buy clothes and DVDs, we literally were in each other's faces twenty-four-seven. My daughter seemed to love every minute of the attention my mother and I were showering her with. But even the cute cuddliness of a little baby wasn't enough to break the monotony. We had been disciplined as hell about not speaking to anyone, but I couldn't take the isolation anymore. It was like we had put ourselves in prison, and I needed to speak to somebody or else I was going to go crazy.

I desperately wanted to call my baby's father just so I could hear his voice. We weren't an official couple or anything, but I did have strong feelings for him, and after all he was my daughter's father and I was sure that he was worried as hell about us. Plus, from a woman's point of view, at least for me anyway, no matter how much strength I pretended to have, there is just something about the strength of a man that I needed to connect with on a regular basis to help me recharge. And there was no other person that I liked recharging with more than Lorenzo.

So my mother finally gave in and let me call Lorenzo on one of our prepaid cell phones. She also decided to call Shanice on one of the other prepaid phones. We had agreed that no matter what, if anybody we spoke to even hinted or mentioned anything about the cop killing or the bank robberies we would just act like we had no idea what the hell they were talking about.

So after we had made our calls and the ten-minute conversations were over, my mother was pissed off at me for telling Lorenzo exactly where we were staying. She saw right through me using my daughter as an excuse; she knew that I really wanted Lorenzo to fly down to see my ass. But she didn't harp on that for too long because she was more concerned about what Shanice had relayed to her.

"Shanice told me that Panama has been blowing up her phone looking for me. All them connections that he had been talking about—well, apparently they came through and he wants to get these guns to make shit happen," my mother said to me, sounding all upbeat and shit.

"So you gonna call him?"

"Chyna, why wouldn't I? It's not like we have much of a choice. This dough that we have ain't gonna last forever, and we still ain't solved that shit with the Bloods so we got moves to make."

I looked at her and reminded her that that the following day I was gonna go through with the plans that we had made for me to start dancing at a strip club in Atlanta called Daydreams. Not only would we be able to use the extra cash, but I knew that by stripping I could start connecting with new people and possibly start on a new hustle.

"Chyna, I still want you to get out there in the clubs, meeting who we need to meet, but right now Panama is talking real shit so we gotta listen," my mother said. She paused, then added, "Yes! I told you his ass was real. We just had to give that nigga some time to get back on his feet. I knew he was gonna get shit poppin' for us."

My mother's mood was the brightest I had seen it in like a month. She scooped up Nina and bounced around the room with her, tickling her and all kinds of happy shit.

When she finished dancing and bouncing around with Nina she called Panama and, sure enough, just when we were on the run and at our weakest moment, he came through with all these major contacts who were miraculously ready to spend all kinds of money.

My mother bought everything that he filled her head up with. She was on the phone cheesing to no end as she spoke to him. "Okay, okay, yes, baby. We gonna make this happen . . . Yeah, I was thinking the same thing . . . No doubt . . . No doubt." That's how some of my mother's conversation with Panama flowed.

All I know is that when my mother's conversation with Panama had ended she started pitching to me about how we could just stay down in Atlanta and let Panama mastermind everything up in New York.

"Chyna, we don't have no fucking choice!" my mother screamed. "If we go back to New York and get knocked we ain't ever gonna see the light of day, and you know that shit."

I hadn't even said anything and my mother was already on the defensive. But at that point we were weak and vulnerable and I knew that we wouldn't be in a strong shot-calling position for some time to come so we had to do what we had to do, even if it meant trying hard to trust Panama and his snake ass.

So as it stood Lorenzo would be flying down to see Nina and me the next day, and according to my mother she wanted Panama and his boys to drive down within a week or so, so that we could get things poppin' and send Panama back to New York with the guns so that he could get that money rolling in for us again.

The next day, which was Friday, the last Friday in September, I called Lorenzo to confirm that he was definitely gonna be flying in to Atlanta that night. He assured me that he was. The thing was, his flight wasn't scheduled to get in until after eleven at night, so I wouldn't be able to pick him up because I had planned on dancing at Daydreams that same night.

And since we were only operating with the used Jetta that we had bought, my mother had agreed to drop me off at the strip club and then head straight to the airport to pick up Lorenzo and bring him back to the apartment. I would see him when I got off.

It had been a little over three weeks since I had seen another human being that I was close to other than my mother and Nina, so I was excited as hell that Lorenzo was coming down. Not to mention that I hadn't had any good dick in a while and I knew that Lorenzo would have no problem breaking me off any, so I was excited about that, too. I think that my excitement was what caused the day to fly by; before I knew it I was kissing my daughter good-bye after my mother had dropped me off at Daydreams.

I had already gone in earlier in the week and met the manager and made arrangements to start dancing there on that Friday. So when I arrived at the club he was happy to see me, and happy that I had followed through on my promise.

"I told you I was coming through," I said and smiled as he walked with me and pointed me in the direction of the dressing room.

"Good, good, you kept your word. I like that. Now, like I was telling you before, it usually gets packed in here at about one in the morning. So you'll make a lot of money, but again, like I told you, it's different down here than it is up in New York."

I smiled and told the owner that I was all too familiar with the Atlanta strip-club scene and that I would be able to hold my own. I knew that in Atlanta it was more like anything goes. Unlike in New York, the dancers in Atlanta are allowed to get butt-ass naked. And besides that, overall it's just a whole other level of freakiness that goes on inside the Atlanta strip clubs as opposed to the ones in New York. But I was ready for it, and I was a professional, so I immediately jumped in the mix and fit right in and started making money.

But by one-thirty in the morning, just as it was

really getting packed, and although I had only made about six hundred dollars thus far, something was telling me that I needed to get dressed and just bounce immediately.

It was like I had gotten shook all of a sudden. I started wondering, what if there were undercover cops walking around in the club who would somehow recognize me from having been on CNN? Then I started kicking myself and beating myself up for having told the owner of the club that I was even from New York. My mind was really bugging. I was thinking crazy thoughts, like, what if the owner had all kinds of violations against the club and he had recognized my face from the news and worked out a deal to rat me out in exchange for the violations on his club being removed? And I also started stressing and wondering, what if the club was to get raided by the vice squad and I got rounded up and arrested with everybody else?

With all those thoughts running through my head, even though I had been drinking and even done a line of coke that one of the other dancers had shared with me, I was still gonna follow my rule of never going against my gut feeling. Whenever my gut told me something and I didn't listen I usually regretted it.

There was no sense in me trying to get all high and liquored up just to avoid stressing about the thoughts that were flowing through my head. So I quickly strolled off to the dressing room and non-chalantly got dressed and got the hell up outta that club. I didn't even wanna call my mother and wait for her to come scoop me up. There were cabs parked outside in front of the club so I just jumped in one of the cabs and had the cabdriver take me back to the apartment.

Not until the cabdriver pulled up to the front of my apartment did I start to feel relieved. My nerves began to calm down. I exhaled and I gave the cab-driver thirty dollars and made my way up to the sec-ond floor of the garden-style apartment complex we were staying in.

As I got right up on the door to our apartment I paused because I had heard an all-too-familiar sound: the sound of my mother hollering the way she does whenever she's getting fucked. My eyes frowned up. I thought to myself for a minute, trying to figure out when exactly my moms said that Panama would be coming down from New York.

But in reality I didn't have to pause and think about shit because my mind knew exactly what the hell was going down. I instantly felt sick to my stomach, like I was gonna throw up, because I knew that it had to be Lorenzo who was in that apartment fucking my mother!

This rage instantly came over me but I calmed myself down enough to slowly and quietly take out my keys so that I could open the door without being heard and catch my mother and Lorenzo in the act.

I managed to get my keys out and unlock the door and slip in the apartment quietly. Although the lights were out, the television provided enough light in the room for me to see just what the hell was going on. And sure enough, right there on the carpeted living room floor, my mother and Lorenzo were both butt-ass naked and going at it doggy-style.

Without hesitating I dropped my bag and my keys on the floor and charged my mother. I grabbed two fists full of her hair and yanked her ass to the ground, ramming her face to the floor. I started wailing on her. For the first time in my life I found myself fighting my mother on some real shit.

"You fucking ho!" I screamed. "How the hell you gonna fuck Lorenzo with my goddamn daughter in the other room?"

Lorenzo was literally shocked like a motherfucker and he was quickly trying to scramble and put on his clothes. He was yelling at me to calm the fuck down, and he was saying that it wasn't nothing.

Meanwhile, my mother was trying her hardest to get to her feet but I knew that if I let her get to her feet she would probably murder me.

"Ma, I can't believe you would do this shit to me!" I screamed while still raging on her. I had never ever been that mad before, and I couldn't believe how enraged I was. The anger I was feeling was actually scaring me.

I heard my daughter start crying from the other room, and that was the only thing that caused me to pause and slow down. And just as I slowed down, Lorenzo, who had managed to get his pants on, came and snatched me off of my mother.

"Your ass is dying tonight, bitch! You put your fucking hands on me like that. Oh, hell no!" my mother yelled. She was standing butt naked and she immediately started heading toward the bedroom that was down the hallway, and I knew that she was going for her gun.

"Get the fuck off of me, Lorenzo," I screamed as I wiggled myself free from his grip. I charged my mother again but I didn't catch her off guard and she spun and punched me dead in my face. We started exchanging blows as if we were in a heavyweight championship fight; we were going at it like two dudes in the street. It wasn't no scratching or slapping—it was straight fists and knuckles. My moms was definitely starting to get the best of me. But I had gotten mines off, too.

Lorenzo managed to step in and separate the two of us, and in the background Nina was screaming like I had never heard her scream before. It was like she knew that me and her grandmother were the ones fighting even though she couldn't physically see us. But even her screams weren't enough to calm me down.

"So you been fucking my mother all this time that you been fucking me?" I screamed at Lorenzo. I also hurled some spit at his ass.

"Chyna, it ain't even like that," my mother shouted. She was still breathing hard from our fight.

"Bitch, shut the fuck up!" I screamed.

I was so amped and so heated. I knew that I had to get outta that apartment or else I would kill my mother. She knew how strong my feelings were for Lorenzo, even though he wasn't ready to just be exclusive with me at that point in our life. My mother had to know that she had crossed the line by fucking him. And I knew that niggas think with they dick so I was definitely blaming my moms more than I was blaming him.

Nina was still screaming her head off in the bedroom, but I didn't even go and check on her. I was just so fucking pissed off that I grabbed my car keys, my bag, and my cell phone and stormed outta the house.

I didn't care about running from the police anymore, I didn't care about making money, and at that point I really didn't care about respecting the game and the code of the streets and all that bullshit.

The way I was looking at it was, if my own damn mother could cross me and not follow codes, then why the hell shouldn't I cross her black ass and send her to jail?

I guess there really isn't any honor among thieves.

12

Shanice

For two days I stayed by myself at a Holiday Inn just outside of Atlanta. My anger was starting to die down, but I just couldn't get the image of my mother backing her ass up into my baby's father's dick out of my head. It made me cringe just thinking about it. I had thought long and hard about calling Lorenzo to curse his ass out but I knew had I called him and found out that he was still in Atlanta fucking my mother I would have flat-out lost it.

I hadn't seen my daughter during those two days that I was in the hotel, and I was hoping that Lorenzo had taken her back to New York with him. But a big part of me knew that since he was always running in the street he would have asked my mother to do him the favor of looking after Nina, and he would have returned to New York solo.

Twice during my stay at the hotel I had picked up the phone and dialed 411 to get the number of the U.S. Attorney's office. And each time I wrote the number down, then I stared at it with sweaty palms for like half an hour straight. I was contemplating if I should call and try to work out a deal with the government that would give me immunity if I were to rat out my moms. After all, she was the one who had physically gone inside the banks and passed those notes, and she was the one who had pulled the trigger in the cop killing. And I was sure that the Feds would be willing to set me and Nina up for life in the Witness Protection Program in exchange for my mother being locked away based on my testimony.

The only thing that held me back from placing that call was that I didn't want the Feds to show up to arrest my mom and then have her try to pull a stunt like holding my daughter hostage to help get her ass out of a sling.

My mother's friend Shanice had practically helped raise me, and she was always a voice of reason, so I knew that before doing anything drastic that I might later regret I should at least reach out to Shanice and chat her up.

I had only the prepaid cell phone on me, and I didn't have Shanice's new cell phone number memorized, so I had to call her on her home phone and hope that she was there. Thankfully she was there; she picked up after the second ring.

"Shanice?"

"Yeah, who's this? Chyna?"

"Yeah."

"Oh my God! Chyna, you had us going crazy. Listen. I don't wanna talk on this phone, but hang up and I'll call you right back at the number that's on the caller ID. Okay?"

I agreed and hung up and waited for Shanice to call me back. And she did call right back.

"Girl, where you been? You got your mother stressed out like I never heard or seen her before—"

I cut Shanice off in the middle of what she was saying and began to curse my mother's name. "Fuck that bitch. I bet you she didn't tell you that I caught her fucking Lorenzo, did she?"

"Yeah, Chyna, actually she did. And that's why she's so stressed out—"

I cut Shanice off again. "Well, she ain't look

stressed out when she was taking all that dick like a damn porno star."

Shanice didn't say anything for a moment and neither did I.

"Chyna, she told me that they were sitting around drinking and smoking weed and the shit just popped off, but it wasn't nothing. It was the liquor and weed that made them do it," Shanice tried to reason on my mother's behalf.

"Fuck that! Shanice, you know and I know that when motherfuckas get drunk they just be doing the shit that they ain't got the guts to do when they sober."

"Chyna, just call her so she can know you're aight, and just hear her out. I'm telling you, I knew Roxy before you was born. And I know she ain't mean nothing behind all this. You know how much she fucking loves you? Chyna, trust me. I *know* your mother."

"You don't fuck your daughter's baby's father if you got love for your daughter. And she was all ghetto about the shit. Fucking the nigga with my daughter right in the other damn room! Ugh. I just wanna choke her ass," I vented to Shanice.

"I don't know what else to tell you, but I can tell

you this shit. The cops is tapping everybody's shit, looking for y'all, and somebody is already snitching on you *and* Roxy. So what you need to do is set this whole shit to the side for a minute and get with your moms and y'all gotta figure out how to get your asses outta the sling y'all in."

I tried calming down and listening to Shanice because I knew that she was right. I had to try hard to put my emotions to the side and think rationally. All those thoughts about the Witness Protection Program and all of that were stemming from emotional thinking, not rational thinking.

When I thought about everything rationally I realized that even if I went to the Feds and snitched, there wasn't nothing guaranteed for my ass—I could end up snitching and not getting anything out of it. Plus, even if I didn't snitch and my mother was to get knocked by the police, it was like her downfall would definitely lead to my downfall. So thinking rationally I knew that me and my moms being united was only gonna benefit both of us, but if we were to stay divided it would be just a matter of time before we both went down.

"Whatchu mean somebody is already snitching?" I asked Shanice.

She went on to explain that the police had been harassing everybody who knows my mother and me. They were rounding people up and taking them in for questioning, and when they'd brought her in they started asking her if she knew anything about the people who had robbed our house and whether or not we were planning on retaliating for that robbery.

"Get the fuck outta here."

"I swear to God."

"So what did you say?"

"I ain't say shit. I told them motherfuckas I ain't know what the fuck they was talking about."

"Shanice, I know P. J. ain't say shit to the police, so that gotta be Panama running his damn mouth."

"Chyna, I just finished telling your mother the exact same thing. But she ain't buying it 'cause she can't see Panama's motive for snitching."

I sighed in utter disbelief. My mother knew how levelheaded and rational Shanice was, so if she ain't believe Shanice's intuition she was definitely in some serious denial.

"Shanice, you don't even know the half about how I been telling my moms I don't trust Panama. She just can't fucking see the shit," I vented.

"Chyna, look, you know I love Roxy to no end.

So understand what I'm about to say. Your mother
does see it, but she's just indebted to Panama because
of the whole history with CSC. And more than that,
though. See, Chyna, your mother probably never told
you this, but he basically took the rap for her on some
shit that went down years ago. People think Panama
simply didn't snitch on Roxy, and yeah, that's true,
he didn't snitch, but it's a whole other level when a
nigga actually *admits* guilt to some shit that he knows
he didn't do. You feel me? So I mean, put yourself
in your mother's position. Like how do you repay a
nigga for some shit like that?"

I hadn't actually ever known all of those details,
so I wouldn't have known to look at it from that
standpoint. But at the same time something still
wasn't adding up.

"But, Shanice, okay, even from that standpoint,
from shit that Lorenzo showed me, to just obvious
shit like when we got robbed that night, dude is still
on some bitch-ass shit and it just don't add up," I
said.

"I know exactly where you coming from. And
this is the thing. All them years in prison where the
nigga was just sitting behind bars rotting away and
your moms and other cats that he knows was on

the outside living it up and not blowing trials, after a while that starts to get to a nigga and eat at him. And I'm telling you, when Panama was sitting in the penitentiary he became bitter and envious as hell. It's like he went in on some ultimate street love and loyalty but after years of being in the system that shit broke his ass down, and I just think he was like *fuck it*. I mean, people grow apart naturally, but when you got prison bars separating you there's this distance that starts to develop really fast. So the first year or two it was all love, everybody was taking his phone calls and going to see him and all of that, but then that shit started to fade and when it did I think that's when Panama's animosity really set in and put him on a path of some revenge-payback shit."

I sat on my hotel bed just shaking my head because it was all starting to make sense to me even though in my heart I just believed that Panama was a snitch from birth. I could see exactly where Shanice was coming from, though. A perfect case in point was the dude Chris Styles—it was like he might as well have been dead. Even though he was in a supermax facility, niggas didn't have no more love for his ass because they knew he was never getting out, so he was a definite case of outta sight, outta mind.

"And Chyna, trust me, your mother and I spoke about this shit so many times. She's just loyal to that nigga, and we can't really knock her until we know what it's like to have somebody take a rap for us and do fifteen years in prison. We don't know how we would react to shit until we put in certain situations."

I blew out some air in disgust because I saw everything coming full circle. Panama's underlying bitterness toward my moms was what was motivating him to want to take over her shit. And now with my mom's back against the wall he was most likely gonna try and capitalize by helping to put her ass behind bars so that she could feel what he'd felt for all those years, being locked up. Not to mention that with my moms out of the picture he wouldn't have to split money with nobody.

"Shanice, my moms done already told Panama the ins and outs of this whole gun hustle. The nigga knew exactly what he was doing. He used my moms, milked her ass for money and for info, and now he's gonna try and take her outta the picture," I reasoned.

Shanice and I were on the same page. And she expressed that she was so glad that I had called because she had a plan to turn the tables on Panama and permanently remove his ass from the picture— but she would need me to help her enact that plan.

Shanice hadn't said nothing but a word.

I was all ears, and I was all in and down for whatever.

By the time me and Shanice got off the phone we had come up with a foolproof plan to play on Panama's snake ass, and to simultaneously kill his ass in the process.

We had to hurry up and checkmate Panama because he was definitely in bed with the cops, which meant that at any moment we could be taken down by the police, and Panama would checkmate us.

13

It's Done

The next day was Monday, October 2nd. I still hadn't spoken to my mother and I was still holed up in the Holiday Inn. But in order to fully carry out the plan that Shanice and I had come up with, I knew that I would have to go by and see my moms and settle the beef I had with her. I was still angry, but I knew it would be in our best interest, and since me and Shanice hadn't hipped my mother to our plan I also had to go see my moms so I could distract her and keep her from calling or speaking to Panama until the plan had been carried out.

After taking a shower and throwing on my clothes I got on my cell phone and called Panama.

"Yo," Panama said as he picked up the phone.

I purposely didn't say anything; I just blew air into the phone in an attempt to play like I was thoroughly disgusted with something.

"Yo. Hello!" Panama yelled into the phone.

"What's up, Panama? This is Chyna," I said in a dejected tone.

"Chyna? What's good, ma?"

"Panama, you see my number on your caller ID? I'm calling you from a prepaid cell phone, and I need you to hang up and call me right back from another phone. Hurry up, though," I said not trusting if Panama's phone was tapped.

"Chyna, what's up?"

I didn't say anything else. I just hung up the phone and waited for Panama to call me back. Sure enough, in less than a minute my cell phone was ringing.

"Chyna?"

"Yeah, what's the deal?"

"You tell me, ma?"

"Well, you know shit is real hot for us right now and I ain't trusting these fucking phones and shit."

"Chyna, you talking to me, come on now, you know my shit is proper. So what's good? Where you at?"

I blew some more air into the phone. I was doing

the perfect acting job. I was coming across like I couldn't care less about anything and everything.

"I'm down south, but I'm fucked up."

"What happened?"

I sucked my teeth and said, "She ain't even say shit to you, did she? See how she do? It figures my moms wouldn't tell you *this* shit . . ."

"What?" Panama asked, and I could tell he was anxious as hell to know what I was getting at.

"Yo, Panama, the other night I come in the crib, right, and I catch my mother with her ass in the air fucking my baby's father. So I flipped the fuck out and me and her got into some shit and started fighting and she was saying she gonna kill me and this and that and yada yada yada. So I was like, fuck it, I'm out. And I just bounced on her ass. And now I'm like I'ma just do me."

"Get the fuck outta here! So your moms is fucking dude?"

"Yeah, and I ain't even know. That's some foul shit, right? I never thought my moms would play me and snake me like that. Not over some dick."

"Chyna, yo, on the real, I know that's your baby's father and all, but it ain't your moms, it's that nigga Lorenzo. He on some bullshit! Trust me when I tell you that the *only* reason I ain't wet his ass is outta respect for your daughter. You knaimean? But just say the word and I'll have his ass chopped up!" Panama promised.

"Nah, we ain't even gotta go there with it. The thing is, I just can't fuck with them if they can cross me and play me like that. But at the same time I know I can't really do this gun hustle without help, so I'm reaching out to you 'cause I need you to help me out on something."

"What's good, ma? Chyna, you know you family."

I went on to explain to Panama how I could help him run guns by making the purchases for him down south if he would arrange for and handle all the deals up north—and I told him that we should do it without my mother.

"Panama, I mean, I know you and my mother go way back and I'm not asking you to snake her or jeopardize what—"

Panama cut me off and told me that I didn't even need to explain shit to him. He knew where I was coming from. "Chyna, your moms is good people. And she's one of the realest out there. Ain't nobody snaking her and ain't nobody snaking nobody. All we gonna do is get this paper and make shit pop off

and to keep it totally one hundred witchu. I already
told your mother I wasn't really gonna be fucking
with her that tight if she was gonna be fucking wit'
ol' boy. You feel me? I mean I got cats ready to put
money in my hands and I need your moms right now
and I wanna eat, but if I can fuck with you and you
telling me dude is out the picture then that's what's
up. Your moms will know that she can slide back to
the table at any time, and we'll all be good just as
long as she leaves them bitch niggas alone. Plus your
moms is so hot right now she don't need to be doing
nothing but hiding out."

I blew more air into the phone and smiled a little
bit. I was hoping that my smile would come through
the phone and help Panama to lower his guard even
more.

"Panama, where you at right now?"

"I'm in Harlem. I spent the night out here."

"Listen, I need you to do me this solid, but you
gotta give me your word you won't fuck me on this."

"Baby girl, come on. You know my stats. Don't
play me like that."

"Okay, I gotta talk quick 'cause my minutes are
almost up on this phone. Matter of fact, if the call
drops give me like a half-hour and I'll call you back."

"Aight, so what's up, though?"

"You seen all the shit that was on the news about the banks and the cops and all that shit—"

"Right, right, that's what I'm saying about Roxy being hot right now. Y'all was on some real gang-stress shit!" Panama said and chuckled.

I chuckled, too. "Yeah, straight Bonnie and Clyde for real for real. But we had to bounce up outta New York real quick, and what we did was we parked my mother's car in this parking garage on the west side near the Lincoln Tunnel so that nobody would be able to track shit. We knew it would be safe in that garage and we didn't wanna be running with all the cash on us so we stashed like twenty grand that we had copped from the banks and it's in the trunk underneath the spare tire."

"Get the fuck outta here."

"Panama, I'm dead-ass!"

I could hear Panama laughing and sounding excited on the other end of the phone, so I kept on.

"We left the remote that'll open up the trunk with Shanice. So I need you to go by her crib and get the remote. She'll give you the address to the parking garage. Get the loot and wire that shit to me and I'll be able to get whatever you need and then all we gotta do is just figure out how to get them shits back up to New York."

"Shanice is home?"

"Yeah, I just spoke to her ass before I called you. But I ain't tell her what I was planning on doing with the cash. She's waiting for you to come get the remote. She ain't question shit 'cause she ain't got no reason to question what we doing, and if she gonna give up the remote to anybody you know she definitely gonna give it up to you."

"Definitely," Panama said.

I could sense that his wheels were turning so I spoke up real quick.

"Just hurry up, though, and go by her crib because I don't want my moms to contact her and then Shanice bring the shit up. You know what I'm saying? And I'm gonna go chat up my moms like I'm on some making-up shit just to keep her occupied."

"No doubt," Panama said.

Before hanging up I told him to roll solo because I didn't want people knowing what was up or what we were holding. He assured me that he had me and that he would get up with me.

So with that part of the plan in place I rushed back over to the apartment, hoping like hell that my mother would be there. On the drive to the apartment I hollered back at Shanice to let her know that Panama had taken our bait.

"Shanice, the nigga is so wide open right now. It's crazy!" I said and I laughed into the phone.

Shanice laughed back and told me that she had to hurry up and go so that she could update P. J.

"You see that nigga's true colors now, right?" Shanice said to me in reference to Panama before hanging up to holla at P. J.

In a way I was kind of surprised at how cold-blooded Shanice and I had been in the plot that we hatched. The thing was, in the streets you need to be cold-blooded, and if you aren't the next man will catch you slippin'. And as far as Panama was concerned, Shanice and I were that next man. And if everything worked out like we'd planned for it to work out, we were just about to catch Panama slippin'.

See, Shanice had already dropped P. J. off at the garage and he was inside the trunk of the BMW with a gun and a silencer, waiting for Panama to open the trunk. And when Panama did open the trunk P. J. was gonna blast his ass and then stuff him inside the same trunk and leave his snitch ass right there to rot.

We knew the plan would work because Panama

had no fucking integrity, and in the end that was gonna be his downfall.

I finally made it back to the apartment. To my surprise, my mother was there but my daughter wasn't.

"Where's Nina?" I asked my mother as I bolted past her, not bothering to say hello.

"Chyna, I was wrong for what I did, but you better fucking show me some more respect than that. Don't just walk past me and not fucking say hello!" my mother screamed at me.

It wasn't even noon yet and I could tell that my mother had been drinking because her speech was kind of slurred and she stumbled when she stood up. Right then and there I knew that she had been stressed out to no end while I was gone. That showed me that she had been distraught about what she had done to me. Or at least that's how I wanted to interpret it.

"Ma, I'll show you some respect. Just tell me where the fuck my daughter is!"

"She went back to New York with Lorenzo," my mother explained.

My mother looked like a hot mess. And I wasn't used to seeing her looking anything less than decked out, even if it was early in the morning.

"Baby, look. I know I fucked up. I know that. And it's been eating my ass up. We got the Feds on our ass, we got the Bloods on our ass, our hustle is fucked up. I ain't never been stressed out like this before in my life!" my mother said to me. As she came closer to me I could smell the liquor on her breath, mixed with the scent of weed.

"Ma, it's aight. We gonna be aight," I said to her.

"We gonna be aight, but we gotta do this shit together, Chyna," my mother replied.

"You right."

"Chyna, it didn't mean shit! I know you saw what you saw and caught us doing what we was doing but it didn't mean shit. I was just drunk and high and stressed out and we hadn't been around no people in like three weeks and—"

I cut my mother off and told her to stop. "Ma, stop. Just stop! You ain't gotta explain nothing. It is what it is. I still respect you. Aight?"

My mother closed her eyes and draped herself around me and gave me a hug. And just as she started hugging me my cell phone began ringing.

"We gonna figure this shit out together and we gonna stay on top together," my mother said to me as I loosened myself from her grip so that I could answer my phone.

HARLEM HEAT

"Chyna, who is that calling you on the phone? You been giving out that prepaid number?"

"Ma it's aight. I got this."

I picked up the phone after it had finished its fourth ring and from the caller ID I knew that it was Shanice.

"It's done," Shanice said.

"It's done?" I asked for confirmation.

"Emptied the whole clip. It's done," Shanice replied coldly.

I smiled a slight but cold-blooded smile.

"Yeah. It's definitely done, then," I said before hanging up the phone.

Fast Forward To
July 2007
New Haven, Connecticut

I hated being in such close proximity to New York and yet not being able to see Nina. It had been months since I'd seen my daughter. In fact, I hadn't seen her since the day I'd caught Lorenzo and my moms fucking. And that was because me and my mother totally wanted to stay off the radar from our past, so we spoke to nobody we had formerly known. But not seeing my daughter was eating at me like you wouldn't believe, and I just couldn't take it anymore. Plus I was bored as hell living a quiet suburban life on the run while hustling E-pills at white clubs in Connecticut and Massachusetts.

"Chyna, I know you wanna see her and that you miss her and I do, too, but I'm telling you, we need to get this new Ecstasy hustle poppin' a little bit more before we send for her," my mother reasoned.

I wasn't trying to hear her and I needed to be with Nina. So against my mother's wishes I contacted Lorenzo. Lorenzo was furious with me for disappearing on him and he screamed at me for about twenty minutes. But I pleaded my case and explained to him that I had done what I did because I had no other choices available to me.

After all Lorenzo's yelling and venting and my explaining my actions, Lorenzo and I arranged to meet at an I-95 rest stop, where I was gonna pick up Nina and take her off his hands. I figured that it would be best to meet at a public and neutral place because it was still too soon for me and my mother to trust anybody with knowing exactly where we were living.

After I met Lorenzo and picked up Nina I couldn't contain myself—I barely made it home without crashing my car because I was constantly turning around to look at Nina while I drove. Although Nina was too young to talk I could tell that had she known how to talk, she would have told me how much she missed me and how much she loved me. I could see it all over her face and in her smile, and I could hear it in the googly noises that she made.

HARLEM HEAT

When I made it home my mother was shocked to see Nina. She was also concerned that I had made contact with Lorenzo, especially since she had finally come to grips with the fact that Panama had been a rat and a snake and now she didn't trust anybody. But probably even more than me, she was so excited to see Nina.

Prior to making it back home, though, I had gone out and bought a bed for Nina, which was gonna be delivered the next day. I also bought her all kinds of toys and clothes and candy and ice cream and anything else I could think of to spoil her with.

That first night that Nina was back at home with us I stayed up with her watching a Barney DVD until she and I both fell asleep on the futon that we had let out into a bed.

We had probably been sleeping for about an hour or so and it was really late, like one in the morning. As I slept I could have sworn that I was having a dream about that all-too-familiar scene from my childhood when my mom came bursting into my room to get the drugs she had stashed under my mattress so that she could flush them down the toilet before the cops found them.

"Chyna! Get up! Get up, girl. Grab Nina! The fucking cops is outside," my mother screamed.

"Huh?" I asked, trying to sit up and gather myself while wiping spit from my mouth.

"Chyna, the cops is about to raid the house!" my mother screamed. She ran off with a huge bag of E-pills and began flushing the pills down the toilet. "Shit. Come on. Come on, come on! Hurry up and go down!" my mother screamed at the toilet bowl in a panic.

I picked up Nina and frantically thought about what I should do as I heard the front door bust wide open under the cops' battering ram. The sound was so loud that it startled Nina awake and she began crying.

"It's okay, baby. You with mommy, mommy is here. I gotchu," I said to Nina in an attempt to calm her down. On the inside I was a nervous wreck and I didn't know what to do as I heard a stampede of cops running up to the second floor of the house, which is where my mother, Nina, and I were weighing our weak options.

My mother came running toward me out of the bathroom with a look as if she was expecting to get direction from me. But I had no answers for her as to what we should do.

"Police! Don't move! Get the fuck on the ground

and let me see your hands!" an officer in riot gear screamed at me as he pointed what looked like a shotgun at my head.

I didn't want to listen to his commands but I had no choice. I slowly sank to my knees and before I could fully lay my body down on the ground another officer yanked Nina from my arms and kicked me face-first into the carpeted floor. Another cop threw my mother to the floor, and they handcuffed us both.

At that instant, as my heart raced, I didn't know exactly what the future held for me or for my mother or, most important, for my daughter. But one thing was for sure: shit didn't look good for any of us. It looked like our run was finally over. The heat that we had brought to Harlem was about to cool off with the quickness.

TURN THE PAGE FOR EXCERPTS
OF MORE G-UNIT BOOKS
by 50 Cent

DERELICT

by 50 Cent
and Relentless
Aaron

Prison: One of the few places on earth where sharks sleep, and where "you reap what you sow."

Т he note that prisoner Jamel Ross attached with his (so-called) urgent request to see the prison psychotherapist was supposed to appear desperate: *"I need to address some serious issues because all I can think about is killing two people when I leave here. Can you help me!"* And that's all he wrote. But even more than the anger, revenge, and redemption Jamel was ready to bring back to the streets, he also had the prison's psych as a target; a target of his lust. And that was a more pressing issue at the moment.

"As far back as I can remember life has been about growing pains," he told her. "I've been through the phases of a liar in my adolescence, a hustler and thug in my teens, and an all-out con man in my twenties. Maybe it was just my instincts to acquire what I considered resources—by whatever means necessary—but it's a shame that once you get away with all of those behaviors, you become good at it, like some twisted type of talent or profession. Eventually even lies feel like the truth . . .

"I had a good thing going with *Superstar*. The magazine. The cable television show. Meeting and commingling with the big-name celebrities and all. I was positioned to have the biggest multimedia company in New York, the biggest to focus on black entertainment exclusively. BET was based in Washington at the time, so I had virtually no competition. Jamel Ross, the big fish in a little pond . . .

"And of course I got away with murder, figuratively, when Angel—yes, the singer with the TV show and all her millions of fans—didn't go along with the authorities, including her mother, who wanted to hit me with child molestation, kidnapping, and other charges. I was probably dead wrong for laying with that girl before she turned eighteen. But Angel was a very grown-up seventeen-year-old. Besides, when I hit it she was only a few months shy from legal. So gimme a break.

"In a strange way, fate came back to get my ass for all of my misdeeds. All of my pimpmania. That cable company up in Connecticut, with more than four hundred stations and fifty-five million subscribers across the country, was purchased by an even larger entity. It turned my life around when that happened; made my brand-new, million-dollar contract null and void. There was no way that I could sue anyone because lawyers' fees are incredible and my company overextended itself with the big celebrations, the lavish spending, and the increased staff; my living expenses, including the midtown penthouse, the car notes, and maintenance for Deadra and JoJo—my two lovers at the time—were in excess of eleven thousand a month. Add that to the overhead at *Superstar* and, without a steady stream of cash flowing, I had an ever-growing monster on my hands.

"One other thing, both Deadra and JoJo became pregnant, so now I would soon have four who depended on me as the sole provider. Funny, all of this wasn't an issue when things were lean. When the sex was good and everyone was kissing my ass. Now, I'm the bad guy because the company's about to go belly-up."

With a little more than two years left to his eighty-four-month stretch, Jamel Ross finally got his wish, to sit and spill his guts to Dr. Kay Edmondson, the psychotherapist at Fort Dix—the federal correctional institution that was a fenced-in forty-acre plot on that much bigger Fort Dix Army Base. Fort Dix was where army reservists came to train, and simultaneously where felons did hard time for crimes gone wrong. With so many unused acres belonging to the government during peace-time, someone imagined that perhaps a military academy or some other type of income-producing entity would work on Fort Dix, as well. So they put a prison there.

The way that Fort Dix was set up was very play it by ear. It was a growing project where rules were implemented along the way. Sure, there was a Bureau of Prisons guidebook with rules and regula-tions for both staff and convicts to follow. However, that BOP guidebook was very boilerplate, and it left the prison administrators in a position in which they had to learn to cope and control some three thousand offenders inside the fences of what was the largest population in the federal system. It was amazing how it all stayed intact for so long.

"On the pound" nicknames were appreciated and accepted since it was a step away from a man's birth name, or "government name," which was the name that all the corrections officers, administrative staff, and of course the courts used when addressing convicts. So on paper Jamel's name was Jamel Ross. On paper, Jamel Ross was not considered to be a person, but a convict with the registration number 40949–054, something like the forty thousandth prisoner to be filtered through the Southern District of New York. The "054" ending was a sort of area code in his prison ID number. He was sentenced by Judge Benison in October of 1997 and committed to eighty-four months—no parole, and three years probation. The conviction was for bank robbery. However, on appeal, the conviction was "adjusted" since there was no conclusive evidence that Jamel had a weapon. Nevertheless, Jamel certainly *did* have a weapon and fully intended to pull off a robbery, with a pen as his weapon. So the time he was doing was more deserved than not.

But regardless of Jamel's level of involvement, it was suddenly very easy for him to share himself since he felt he had nothing to lose. It was that much easier to speak to a reasonably attractive woman, as if there were good reasons for the things he did and why. So he went on explaining all of his dirty deeds to "Dr. Kay" Edmondson as if this were a confessional where he'd be forgiven for his sins. And why not? She was a good-listening, career-oriented female. She was black and she wasn't condescending like so many other staff members were. And when she called him "Jamel," as opposed to "Convict Ross," it made him imagine they had a tighter bond in store.

"So this dude—I won't say his name—he let me in on his check game. He explained how one person could write a check for, say, one hundred grand, give it to a friend, and even if the money isn't there to back up the check, the depositor could likely withdraw money on it before it is found to be worthless. It sounded good. And I figured the worst-case scenario would be to deny this and to deny that . . ."

"They don't verify the check? I mean, isn't that like part of the procedure before it clears?" Kay generally did more talking than this when convicts sat before her. Except she was finding his story, as well as his in-depth knowledge of things, so fascinating.

"See, that's the thing. If the check comes from the

same region, or if it's from the other side of the world, it still has to go through a clearing house, where all of the checks from *all* of the banks eventually go. So that takes like a couple of days. But banks—certain banks—are on some ol' 'we trust you' stuff, and I guess since they've got your name and address and stuff, they do the cash within one or two days."

"Really?"

"Yup. They will if it's a local check from a local bank. And on that hundred grand? The bank will let loose on the second day. I'll go in and get the money when the dam breaks . . ."

"And when the bank finds out about the check being no good?"

"I play dumb. I don't know the guy who wrote the check. Met him only twice, blah blah blah. I sign this little BS affidavit and *bang*—I'm knee deep in free money."

Dr. Kay wagged her head of flowing hair and replied, "You all never cease to amaze me. I mean *you*, as in the convict here. I hear all sorts of tricks and shortcuts and—"

"Cons. They're cons, Dr. Kay."

"Sure, sure . . ." she somehow agreed.

"But it's all a dead end, ya know? Like, once you

get money, it becomes an addiction, to the point that you forget your *reasons* and *objectives* for getting money in the first place."

"Did *you* forget, Jamel?"

"Did I? I got *so deep* in the whole check thing that it became my new profession."

"Stop playin'."

"I'm for real. I started off with my own name and companies, but then, uh . . ." Jamel hesitated. He looked away from the doctor. "I shouldn't really be tellin' you this. I'm ramblin'."

"You don't have to if you don't want to, but let me remind you that what you say to me in our sessions is confidential, unless I feel that you might cause harm to yourself or someone else, or if I'm subpoenaed to testify in court."

"Hmmm." Jamel deliberated on that. He wondered if the eighty-four month sentence could be enhanced to double or triple, or worse. He'd heard about the nightmares, how bragging while in prison was a tool that another prisoner could use to shorten his own sentence. "Informants" they called them. And just the *thought* of that made Jamel promise himself that he wouldn't say a thing about the weapon and the real reason he caught so much time.

"Off the record, Jamel . . ."

"Oooh, I like this 'off-the-record' stuff." Jamel rubbed his hands together and came to the edge of the couch from his slouched position.

"Well, to put your mind at ease, I haven't *yet* received a subpoena for a trial."

Jamel took that as an indication of secrecy and that he was supposed to have confidence in her. But he proceeded with caution as he went on explaining about the various bank scams, the phony licenses, and bogus checks.

The doctor said, "Wow, Jamel. That's a hell of a switch. One day you're a television producer, a publisher, and a ladies' man, and the next—"

The phone rang.

"I'm sorry." Dr. Kay got up from her chair, passed Jamel, and circled her desk. It gave him a whiff of her perfume and that only made him pay special attention to her calves. There was something about a woman's calves that got him excited. Or didn't. But Dr. Kay's calves *did*. As she took her phone call, Jamel wondered if she did the StairMaster bit, or if she ran in the mornings. Maybe she was in the military like most of these prison guards claimed. Was she an aerobics instructor at some point in her life? All of those ideas were flowing like sweet Kool-Aid in Jamel's head as he thought and wondered and imagined.

"Could you excuse me?" Dr. Kay said.

"Sure," said Jamel, and he quickly stepped out of the office and shut the door behind him. Through the door's window he tried to cling to her words. It seemed to be a business call, but that was just a guess. A hope. It was part of Jamel's agenda to guess and wonder what this woman or that woman would be like underneath him, or on top of him. After all, he was locked up and unable to touch a female being. So his imaginings were what had guided him during these seven years. He'd take time to look deep into a woman, and those thoughts weren't frivolous but anchored and supported by his past. Indeed, sex had been a major part of his life since he was a teen. It had become a part of his lifestyle. Women. The fine ones. The ones who weren't so fine, but whom he felt he could "shape up and get right." Dr. Kay was somewhere in between those images. She had a cute face and an open attitude. Her eyes smiled large and compassionate. She was cheeky when she smiled, with lips wide and supple. Her teeth were bright and indicated good hygiene.

And Dr. Kay wasn't built like an *Essence* model

or a dancer in a video. She was a little thick where it mattered, and she had what Jamel considered to be "a lot to work with." Big-breasted and with healthy hips, Dr. Kay was one of a half dozen women on the compound who were black. There were others who were Hispanic and a few more who were white. But of those who were somehow accessible, Dr. Kay nicely fit Jamel's reach. And to reach her, all he had to do was make the effort to trek on down to the psychology department, in the same building as the chapel and the hospital. All you had to do was express interest in counseling. Then you had to pass a litmus test of sorts, giving your reason for needing counseling. Of course, Dr. Kay wasn't the only psychotherapist in the department. There were one or two others. So Jamel had to hope and pray that his interview would 1) be with Dr. Kay Edmondson, and 2) that his address would be taken sincerely, not as just another sex-starved convict who wanted a whiff or an eyeful of the available female on the compound.

Considering all of that, Jamel played his cards right and was always able to have Dr. Kay set him up for a number of appointments. It couldn't be once a week; the doctor-convict relationship would quickly burn out at that rate. But twice a month was a good start, so that she could get a grip on who (and what) he was about. Plus, his visits wouldn't be so obvious as to raise any red flags with her boss, who, as far as Jamel could tell, really didn't execute any major checks and balances of Kay's caseload. Still, it was the other prisoners at Fort Dix who Jamel had to be concerned about. They had to be outsmarted at every twist and turn, since they were the very people (miserable, locked-up, and jealous) who would often jump to conclusions. Anyone of these guys might get the notion, the hint, or the funny idea that Dr. Kay was getting too personal with one prisoner. Then the dime dropping and the investigation would begin.

BLOW

by 50 Cent
and K'wan

"The game is not for the faint of heart, and if you choose to play it, you better damn well understand the rules."

Prince sat in the stiff wooden chair totally numb. The tailored Armani suit he had been so proud of when he dropped two grand on it now felt like a strait jacket. He spared a glance at his lawyer who was going over his notes with a worried expression on his face. The young black man had fought the good fight, but in the end it would be in God's hands.

He tried to keep from looking over his shoulder, but he couldn't help it. There was no sign of Sticks, which didn't surprise him. For killing a police officer they were surely going to give him the needle, if he even survived being captured. The police had dragged the river but never found a body. Everyone thought

Sticks was dead, but Stone said otherwise. Sticks was his twin, and he would know better than anyone else if he was gone. Prince hoped that Stone was right and wished his friend well wherever fate carried him.

Marisol sat two rows behind him, with Mommy at her side looking every bit of the concerned grandmother. It was hard to believe that she was the embodiment of death, cloaked in kindness. This was the first time he had seen Mommy since his incarceration, but Marisol had been there every day for the seven weeks the trail had gone on. She tried to stay strong for her man, but he could tell that the ordeal was breaking her down. Cano had sent word through her that he would be taken care of, but Prince didn't want to be taken care of; he wanted to be free.

Keisha sat in the last row, quietly sobbing. She had raised the most hell on the day the police came for him, even managing to get herself tossed into jail for obstruction of justice. She had always been a down bitch, and he respected her for it.

Assembled in the courtroom were many faces. Some were friends, but most were people from the neighborhood that just came to be nosey. No matter their motive the sheer number would look good on his part in the eyes of the jury, at least that was what his lawyer had told him. The way the trial seemed to be going, he seriously doubted it at that point.

Lined up to his left were his long-time friends, Daddy-O and Stone. Daddy-O's face was solemn. His dress shirt was pinned up at the shoulder covering the stump where his left arm used to be. It was just one more debt that he owed Diego that he'd never be able to collect on. Stone smirked at a doodling he had done on his legal pad. Prince wasn't sure if he didn't understand the charges they were facing or just didn't care. Knowing Stone, it was probably the latter. He had long ago resigned himself to the fact that he was born into the game and would die in it.

Prince wanted to break down every time he thought how his run as a boss had ended. To see men that you had grown to love like family take the stand and try to snatch your life to save their own was a feeling that he wouldn't wish on anyone. *No man above the team* was the vow that they had all taken, but in the end only a few kept to it. To the rest, they were just words. They had laughed, cried, smoked weed, and got pussy together, but when the time came to stand like men they laid down like bitches. These men had been like his brothers, but that was before the money came into the picture.

6 months earlier

"Come on Daddy-O, you know me." The young man reminded him, not believing that he'd been turned down. He could already feel the sweat trickling down his back and didn't know how much longer he could hold out.

Daddy-O popped a handful of sunflower seeds in his mouth. He expertly extracted the seed using only his tongue and let the shells tumble around in his mouth until he could feel the salty bite. "My dude, why are you even talking to me about this; holla at my young boy," he nodded at Danny.

"Daddy, you know how this little nigga is; he wouldn't let his mama go for a short, so you know I ain't getting a play."

"Get yo money right and we won't have a problem," Danny told him, and went back to watching the block.

"Listen," the young man turned back to Daddy-O. A thin film of sweat had begun to form on his nose. "All I got is ten dollars on me, but I need at least two to get me to the social security building in the morning. Do me this solid, and I swear I'll get you right when my check comes through."

Daddy-O looked over at Danny, who was giving the kid the once-over. He was short and thin with braids that snaked down the back of his neck. Danny had one of those funny faces. It was kind of like he looked old, but young at the same time . . . if that makes sense.

There was a time when Danny seemed like he had a bright future ahead of him. Though he wasn't the smartest of their little unit, he was a natural at sports. Danny played basketball for Cardinal Hayes High School and was one of the better players on the team. His jump shot needed a little fine-tuning, but he had a mean handle. Danny was notorious for embarrassing his opponents with his wicked cross-over. Sports was supposed to be Danny's ticket out, but as most naïve young men did, he chose Hell over Heaven.

For as talented as Danny was physically, he was borderline retarded mentally. Of course not in a literal sense, but his actions made him the most dimwitted of the crew. While his school chums were content to play the roll of gangstas and watch the game from afar, Danny had to be in the thick of it. It was his fascination with the game that caused him to drop out of school in his senior year to pursue his dreams of being a *real nigga*, or a real nigga's sidekick. Danny was a yes-man to the boss, and under the boss is where he would earn his stripes. He didn't really have the heart of a solider, but he was connected to some stand-up dudes, which provided him with a veil of protection. The hood knew that if you fucked with Danny, you'd have to fuck with his team.

"Give it to him, D," Daddy-O finally said.

Danny looked like he wanted to say something, but a stern look from Daddy-O hushed him. Dipping his hand into the back of his pants, Danny fished around until he found what he was looking for. Grumbling, he handed the young man a small bag of crack.

The young man examined the bag and saw that it was mostly flake and powder. "Man, this ain't nothing but some shake."

"Beggars can't be choosers; take that shit and bounce," Danny spat.

"Yo, shorty you be on some bullshit," the young man said to Danny. There was a hint of anger in his voice, but he knew better than to get stupid. "One day you're gonna have to come from behind Prince and Daddy-O's skirts and handle your own business."

"Go ahead wit that shit, man," Daddy-O said, cracking another seed.

"No disrespect to you, Daddy-O, but shorty got a big mouth. He be coming at niggaz sideways, and it's only on the strength of y'all that nobody ain't rocked him yet."

"Yo, go head wit all that *rocking* shit, niggaz know where I be," Danny said, trying to sound confident. In all truthfulness he was nervous. He loved the rush of being in the hood with Daddy-O and the team, but didn't care for the bullshit that came with it. Anybody who's ever spent a day on the streets knows that the law of the land more often than not is violence. If you weren't ready to defend your claim, then you needed to be in the house watching UPN.

The young man's eyes burned into Danny's. "Imma see you later," he said, never taking his eyes off Danny as he backed away.

"I'll be right here," Danny said confidently. His voice was deep and stern, but his legs felt like spaghetti. If the kid had rushed him, Danny would have had no idea what to do. He would fight if forced, but it wasn't his first course of action. Only when the kid had disappeared down the path did he finally force himself to relax.

"Punk-ass nigga," Danny said, like he was bout that.

"Yo, why you always acting up?" Daddy-O asked.

"What you mean, son?" Danny replied, as if he hadn't just clowned the dude.

"Every time I turn around your ass is in some shit, and that ain't what's up."

Danny sucked his teeth. "Yo, son was trying to stunt on me, B. You know I can't have niggaz coming at my head that way."

"Coming at your head?" Daddy-O raised his eyebrow. "Nigga, he was short two dollars!"

"I'm saying . . ."

"Don't say nothing," Daddy-O cut him off. "We out here trying to get a dollar and you still on your schoolyard bullshit. You need to respect these streets if you gonna get money in them," Daddy-O stormed off leaving Danny there to ponder what he had said.

■

The intense heat from the night before had spilled over to join with the morning sun and punish anyone who didn't have air conditioning, which amounted to damn near the whole hood being outside. That morning the projects were a kaleidoscope of activity. People were drinking, having water fights, and just trying to sit as still as they could in the heat. Grills were set up in front of several buildings, sending smoke signals to the hungry inhabitants.

Daddy-O bopped across the courtyard between 875 and 865. He nodded to a few heads as he passed them, but didn't really stop to chat. It was too damn hot, and being a combination of fat and black made you a target for the sun's taunting rays. A girl wearing boy shorts and a tank-top sat on the bench enjoying an ice-cream cone. She peeked at Daddy-O from behind her pink sunglasses and drew the tip of her tongue across the top of the ice cream.

"Umm, hmm," Daddy-O grumbled, rubbing his large belly. In the way of being attractive, Daddy-O wasn't much to look at. He was a five-eight brute with gorilla-like arms and a jaw that looked to be carved from stone. Cornrows snaked back over his large head and stopped just behind his ears. Though some joked that he had a face that only a mother could love, Daddy-O had swagger. His gear was always up, and he was swift with the gift of gab, earning him points with the ladies.

Everybody in the hood knew Daddy-O. He had lived in the Frederick Douglass houses for over twelve years at that point. He and his mother had moved there when he was seven years old. Daddy-O had lived a number of places in his life, but no place ever felt like Douglass.

Daddy-O was about to head down the stairs toward 845 when he heard his name being called. He slowed, but didn't stop walking as he turned around. Shambling from 875 in his direction was a crack head that they all knew as Shakes. She tried to strut in her faded high-heeled shoes, but it ended up as more of a walk-stumble. She was dressed in a black leotard that looked like it was crushing her small breasts. Shakes had been a'ight back in her day, but she didn't get the memo that losing eighty pounds and most of your front teeth killed your sex appeal.

"Daddy-O, let me holla at you for a minute," she half slurred. Shakes's eyes were wide and constantly scanning as if she was expecting someone to jump out on her. She stepped next to Daddy-O and whispered in his ear, "You holding?"

"You know better than that, ma. Go see my little man in the building," he said, in a pleasant tone. Most of the dealers in the neighborhood saw the crack heads as being something less than human and treated them as such, but not Daddy-O. Having watched his older brother and several of his other relatives succumb to one drug or another, Daddy-O understood it better than most. Cocaine and heroin were the elite of their line. Boy and Girl, as they were sometimes called, were God and Goddess to those foolish enough to be enticed by their lies. They had had the highest addiction rate, and the most cases of relapses. Daddy-O had learned early that a well-known crack head could be more valuable to you than a member of your team, if you knew how to use them.

"A'ight, baby, that's what it is," she turned to walk away and almost lost her balance. In true crack head form, she righted herself and tried to strut even harder. "You need to call a sista sometime," she called over her shoulder.

Daddy-O shook his head. There wasn't a damn thing he could call Shakes but what she was, a corpse that didn't know it was dead yet. Daddy-O continued down the stairs and past the small playground. A group of kids were dancing around in the elephant-shaped sprinkler tossing water on each other. One of them ran up on Daddy-O with a half filled bowl, but a quick threat of an ass whipping sent the kid back to douse one of his friends with the water. Stopping to exchange greetings with a Puerto Rican girl he knew, Daddy-O disappeared inside the bowels of 845.